GW00507015

Visitors

Visitors

John Stewart

SHEPHEARD-WALWYN (PUBLISHERS) LTD

© John Stewart 2007

All rights reserved. No part of this book may be
reproduced in any form without the written permission
of the publisher, Shepheard-Walwyn (Publishers) Ltd
www.shepheard-walwyn.co.uk

First published in 2007 by
Shepheard-Walwyn (Publishers) Ltd
15 Alder Road
London SW14 8ER

British Library Cataloguing in Publication Data
A catalogue record of this book
is available from the British Library

ISBN: 978-0-85683-253-6

Typeset by Alacrity, Chesterfield, Sandford, Somerset
Printed through s|s|media limited, Wallington, Surrey

In memory of
Joan Crammond

Acknowledgements

My thanks to Tommas Graves and David Triggs who, from the beginning, offered very real encouragement and also to my publisher Anthony Werner for his guidance and enthusiasm. Brian Hodgkinson's help with historical detail was much appreciated, as was the discerning advice of Addie Morrow. I am also most grateful to Jean Desebrock for her careful editing.

Contents

Prologue

'The resistance level is much higher, Captain.'

'Yes, we're down to interplanetary mode. When travelling within crowded planetary systems, intergalactic or even inter stellar modes are much too dangerous.'

'We must be getting close, Sir.'

'We are, Cadet Alpha. Your English is good, congratulations.'

'Thank you, Sir, the ban on any other language has been a good incentive.'

The Captain chuckled.

'Look at that, Sir!'

'That's Saturn and her frosty rings.'

'How many times have you been to the planet called Earth, Sir?'

'This is the third time. The first time I was, like you, a cadet. But this is the first time we will be showing ourselves.'

'Will it be dangerous?'

'Tricky maybe, but not dangerous. I studied British history at university: their law forbids assault and imprisonment without due process. As long as we keep calm we'll be all right.'

'But why are we showing ourselves?'

'The Chief Elder says, and I agree, that it is unlawful to take without giving. We have taken for a long time, now it is time to give.'

'But they don't know we've been taking!'

'That is irrelevant: the law will not be mocked.'

'Sorry, Sir!'

'Don't be sorry. It is good to speak your mind, for in doing so thoughts can be refined. It is one Universe and an insular tribal attitude is inappropriate. Look, do you see that bright spot in front of us?'

'Yes, Sir.'

'Well that's it; that's the Earth.'

'It's coming up pretty fast!'

'Yes, it's time for approach mode.'

The Cadet watched fascinated as the Earth grew slowly and revealed its beauty.

'It's amazing, Sir, a jewel without a rival! How did we find it in the first place?'

'Many years ago our most renowned Chief Elder told us where to look.'

'How did he know?'

'He knew. That is all we know!'

Chapter One

Visitors from a distant planet unexpectedly arrived. These people had enormous power and our puny defensive systems they neutralised with ease. They told us repeatedly that they'd come in peace and would quickly leave once they had observed our current modes of government and philosophy. The Military who first interviewed them were incredulous and found it difficult to believe, as no space vehicle had been revealed. They explained that they weren't permitted to expose their craft. We didn't believe them and they patiently repeated their story, but never were there any hints of violence. There were no laws that set down rules of how they might be treated, so they were housed like any immigrants who entered by illegal means. On the morning when the news first broke, the Government treated the matter as a fanciful rumour and awaited confirmation, but the Prime Minister, who was at a European summit, called a Cabinet meeting and rushed home.

The Aliens were strangely similar to the human form but their eyes had something special: a deep pool-like tranquillity. Clearly their intellectual and perceptive abilities were of a most advanced nature. Yet they behaved with disarming modesty. They made no complaints about the Spartan nature of their quarters, nor did they make demands or seek a meeting with authority. They merely awaited events.

The media rush was almost instant, but when the TV icons interviewed these beings they simply could not match their intellect. Aggressive questioning had no impact and rebounded upon the questioner. Interest grew, as did respect. Still, many felt that they were simply frauds, and fears of an Alien takeover persisted. The rumour that the small research group were just the herald of a harsh invasion gathered pace. On the streets special-edition newspapers whipped up tensions. The Share Index plummeted and the Stock Exchange closed trading.

By midday opposition leaders and the popular press were demanding action. Their campaign bordered on the hysterical and the Prime Minister Bob Shaw, a square-framed Baldwin-like figure, booked airtime on all the TV channels. This time he would ask the questions!

∗

At 6.30pm the cameras beamed in on the familiar Downing Street scene and right on time the Prime Minister and the Alien leader took their seats – easy chairs placed on either side of the ornate fireplace. The PM was not one you'd call well dressed. His suit always looked as if it needed pressing, but a discerning eye might guess that, even if it had been newly pressed, it would still have had the familiar office-worn appearance.

The Alien's tall trim frame was suited as if by Savile Row. Nothing stood out, although he didn't quite look British. When he removed his tinted glasses though, his eyes betrayed his special nature.

∗

'May I first welcome you on behalf of Her Majesty and the peoples of this island, and may I apologise for this tardy official greeting.' The Prime Minister's words were measured and calm.

'You are most gracious, Prime Minister,' the Alien acknowledged easily.

Shaw was shocked but was too good a 'pro' to show it. The urbanity of this being was amazing.

'Sir, Your English is so *English* that I'm tempted to ask what UK university you attended.'

The Alien laughed easily.

'That is a compliment, Prime Minister, and I do like your English sense of humour!'

'May I ask your name? For I must confess no one was able to tell me. In fact I don't think we enquired! As you may imagine, we were rather taken by surprise!'

'I must apologise for we did arrive unannounced!' The Alien smiled disarmingly. 'Now, my name – I am the leader of a small band of ten. You can call me Captain. My own name is of little matter.'

'Well, Captain, you will be aware that many of our citizens are anxious that your visit may be the herald of a larger force. They clamour for assurances and I must say that I understand their

4

fears. Sir, can we be reassured? And, Sir, where is your space-craft? No one has reported a sighting!'

'I appreciate your candour, Prime Minister. I can only say that your fears are groundless.' The captain smiled. 'Sir, few of our citizens are anxious to leave their planet paradise for what is, to say the very least, a long and tedious, if not uncertain, journey. We may have mastered many of Creation's laws but not them all! Now, you asked about our spacecraft: it is close, should we need to be evacuated, but is protected by an invisibility screen and fitted with a high-pitched sound to repel living creatures. We are forbidden to cause harm or injury and, as our craft is specially protected, even touching it can be dangerous!' The Alien smiled again.

Shaw was amazed: this man, creature, or whatever he was, could grace the high table at any Oxford college.

'Well, Captain, you have answered my questions. Thank you, your word is good enough for me.'

'Prime Minister, your great financial City says it for me: "My word is my bond."'

'How, Sir, do you know our language and our customs so well? To me, your grasp of things is quite uncanny.'

'Over many ages we developed a facility for near to instant assimilation. It is really not so difficult as it seems. A lake that is completely still allows a perfect reflection. So it is with the mind. Let's put it another way. While you have developed the computer, quite miraculously, we have developed aids that advance the felicity of the mind. We didn't show ourselves immediately but gave ourselves a little time to watch and listen. "Cramming" is the word I think you use! Sir, we have come to your planet to learn, and hopefully to be of use.' The Alien smiled benignly but gave no further explanation.

Shaw also smiled but thought it prudent not to follow up. Instead he asked another question.

'You referred to your "Planet Paradise": are the terrain and climate similar to here?'

'Remarkably similar. Life forms such as us need rather special conditions, so it's not surprising therefore that con-ditions are alike. Though we lead a much more simple life.'

Prime Minster Shaw nodded pensively. Questions were crowding his mind, but being prime-time coverage he was circumspect. The main aim was to calm the agitation in the people. The arrival of beings from another planet was momentous; even so, it was business as usual. This he saw to be a premier duty. That said, there was a unique opportunity to learn from these remarkable beings. Had we the capacity though? That was the question.

In the meantime Shaw kept his questions simple and straightforward. Did they like the food? Were their sleeping habits similar? Were their family customs similar?

The Alien's answers were completely disarming. Indeed this was exactly what the PM wanted. The people would be reassured. These Visitors didn't pose a threat and we should treat them as honoured guests. Tomorrow it would be business as usual! That was his hope, but he had been in public life too long to be complacent. There would be trouble. It was inevitable and it would need his every ounce of subtlety to thwart the wreckers.

The Prime Minister's probing continued to emphasise the brevity of the Aliens' stay and their lack of aggression. Indeed the nation stood to gain much from the knowledge the Visitors were so generously sharing. It was good diplomatic stuff. 'Repeat your message three times', his father had told him. 'If you're lucky, they might get it on the third hearing!'

✻

When Shaw was perfectly sure all recording apparatus was disconnected, he leaned across to his visitor.

'Now we can talk!' he said quietly.

The Alien smiled knowingly. Clearly he understood the political subtlety.

'I hope it is convenient for you to dine with us this evening. My wife is busy preparing things and we trust the food will be to your liking. If not, we would fully understand, of course. So there's no need to suffer in the cause of diplomacy!'

The Visitor laughed lightly

'Mr Shaw, I am honoured, not least by the trust you're showing in this creature from another world. But then, this is Britain!' The Visitor's smile widened.

'Poor old Britain, assailed by never-ending rules and regulations – not to mention the tyranny of the PC vigilantes. Sorry, I'm assailing you with obscurities!'

'No, I understand. Your democracy is feeding the popular will with all that it demands, instead of what it needs.'

'Good Lord! How do you know such things? And how have you mastered the English language so completely?'

'This isn't the first mission to your planet, but it's the first to declare itself. We've had ample time to study your customs.'

'Even so, you facility is remarkable. I think it's time to go upstairs to the flat. My wife will be waiting.'

Chapter Two

The Captain was impressed and said so. Here he was alone with the Prime Minister and his wife, and not another witness present. This was trust indeed and marked a man with faith in his perception.

Initial conversation centred on the families of the hosts and guest; it was very much as if the Vicar had come round to supper. Eventually Shaw's curiosity could not be contained.

'Presiding over a Cabinet discussion on the Budget I find purgatorial.'

'Ah, you've got me on that word!'

'I've scored one at last!' Shaw chuckled while giving the meaning. 'How do you deal with the nightmare of taxation?' he questioned.

'You may find this difficult to imagine, but we don't have taxation as such. We have rent-collection centres and, when there is a special need, donations are invited which often build up a reserve well above the immediate requirement.'

'But how do you pay for education and health services?'

'We have no government-funded health or education service. There are centres for those unable to help themselves, but there the need is small.'

'But how...?' Shaw was baffled. 'The need for welfare funds to combat poverty... How...?'

'There may be simplicity – that is mostly by choice – but there is little poverty, and those who are in poverty are mostly those who cannot help themselves.'

'I am totally baffled. You cannot be a primitive, simplistic society, for people who can send heralds halfway across the universe are the very opposite!' Shaw shook his head. 'How do you do it? Your citizens must be uncommonly advanced.'

'And you must have a powerful belief system,' Mrs Shaw interjected.

'Yes, faith is often needed, but truth transcends all.'

To Mrs Shaw the gentle eyes of the Visitor said it all, and she had no doubt that what he said was so.

The Prime Minster was reflective. This man was not a charlatan. He would bet his life on that. But what of war and strife: had they banished that? There had to be a snag somewhere!

'What about criminal activity? How do you deal with disruptive elements? What about war?'

'Constant vigilance is the only answer, and when it's spotted crime must never walk abroad unpunished.'

'And war?' Shaw pressed.

'War happens when a tyrant thinks he sees an easy victory. So prudence and vigilance are essential. Complacency, in this respect, *is* criminal!'

The Captain wasn't a dewy-eyed tree-hugger, Shaw concluded quickly.

'I'm still puzzled by your system of collecting revenue,' he added.

The Visitor smiled. 'Can I ask you a question?'

'Of course.'

'How valuable is the land on which your great financial city rests?'

'Unbelievably valuable!'

'Who collects the value?'

'The landlords.'

'And who creates this value?'

Deep in his memory Shaw trawled up a conversation he once had had with someone on the hustings. He had dismissed it then for he had seen no votes in it. Now the import of it all rushed back.

'Your question: who creates the rent? Everyone who works there; the whole community,' he answered.

'As you say here, that would be a tidy sum!'

'Very tidy! I remember now, my experts told me that this idea was "old hat".'

'"Old hat"?'

'That's another one!'

The Captain laughed

'They meant out of date.'

'Natural law is never out of date.'

'Oh dear, the academics won't like that. "Natural" is "out"!'

9

'Tell them that Nature says it's *in!*'

Shaw and his wife laughed heartily.

'This is a most enjoyable evening, Prime Minister. Laughter is so healthy!'

'Captain, I know what the objectors will say. When collecting the rent, what about the twentieth floor?' Shaw continued.

'We have the same thing, but the twentieth floor is of no concern to the rent-collecting service. They are only interested in the person or body who holds the title to the land area; for, no matter how sophisticated, the building rests on land. In your case it would be the freehold owner. You even have a name for it: ground rent. We have long since rid ourselves of those lingering vestiges of land ownership but you still have leases, sub-leases and so on. Such factors cause interim difficulties but they would soon settle down.'

'And ground rent funds the working of the state?'

'Yes, except for emergencies, as already mentioned.'

'Captain, I find it difficult to credit. Welfare is such a massive burden!'

'When men's labour is free of tax it brings about a revolution and, when those with enterprise have easy access to a business site, commerce mushrooms. People are working as free men. Believe me, it makes a huge difference. The welfare burden will shrink, the education bill will shrink, and citizens at last will have the dignity of choosing their health care and their children's education. They'll be no longer in receipt of charity, or have the anxiety of cruel waiting lists. Charity breeds dependence, but give the people justice and they will rise to it.'

'Captain, this is all very well in the long term, or for yourselves who have had it in place perhaps for many decades, but we by necessity must proceed slowly. Immediate implementation would be a tyranny!'

'Having observed your system, it would take years to introduce on a significant scale. Yet it is the natural system. No other way can you avoid the basic cause of poverty in this age. The old manorial system that my ancestors once observed is past.'

Shaw was once more shocked. Had they been visiting Earth since the Middle Ages? Who were these people? He had much more to learn.

'Clearly, Captain, yours is a race of great achievement. Why then have you shown such continuing interest in our planet?

10

For, as you've just said, you were observing us in the medieval period.'

'We owe you much for you have a genius when it comes to spiritual insight,' the Captain answered quietly. 'Even now, your enlightened ones preach the unity of spirit that unites us all. Yes, we learned much, and we wish to show our gratitude.'

Shaw waited for the Captain to elaborate but he remained silent. Eventually it was Mrs Shaw who spoke.

'How do you intend to act, Sir?'

'We have no plans. We can respond to questions but that is all. As you say in your military circles, it's our rules of engagement.' The countenance of the Visitor seemed even more benign.

'What questions do you think we should be asking?'

The Visitor laughed.

'You're not a politician for nothing, Mr Shaw.'

'I continue to be amazed at your facility with our language and the idiom – well, that is really amazing!'

'Britain was my subject at what you would call university.'

'Now, Sir, what have we forgotten? What does this country need?'

'The centre, the core of certainty is being eroded. We have watched this disturbing trend with sadness.'

'This, and the fanatical counter-trend burning in the Muslim states, concern me greatly, but every time I speak I'm shredded by the media.'

'"Shredded"? – Yes, I get the meaning! Does the shredding worry you?'

'If it did I would be dead.'

'Keep speaking, Sir. You'll be planting seeds and they will grow. Britain is a fertile land.'

Chapter Three

The House of Commons was packed. All the seats were occupied and there were many standing on the floor by the Speaker's chair and by the entrance to the lobby. In the gallery the Lords were assembled. The buzz of conversation was feverish. Then suddenly a hush descended. The Prime Minister had arrived exactly on time.

'The Prime Minister...' the Speaker intoned and Bob Shaw rose to his feet.

'Mr Speaker, My Lords and Ladies and Honourable Members, this is indeed a momentous day and we have perhaps the biggest television audience this place has ever drawn. So I hope you will behave yourselves!'

There was a ripple of obliging chuckles.

'We are indeed honoured by the presence of our guests and awed by their achievements in travelling from their distant planet. Now, I must tell you that this is not the first time they have visited us. On other occasions they did not show themselves but this time they have. I must emphasise that at no time have they shown aggression or caused harm to this planet. Their interest has been in our customs and in our genius for spiritual and philosophical penetration, and for this they said they were eternally grateful. So I don't think that this is something the MOD need see as an emergency.'

An MP stood up and Shaw gave way.

'Who were the philosophers and spiritual leaders the Alien mentioned?'

'The captain of the Visitors dined at Downing Street last evening. My good wife did the cooking and it was a most pleasant evening. Afterwards I accompanied him to his MOD quarters and on the journey he listed those that he had studied: Plato, the Johannine Gospel and the Brahmins of India. He was also much entertained by the writings of the Sufi master Rumi. He also named the Chinese Taoist master Chuang Tzu. I'm ashamed to say he knew much more than I. Now, I'm sorry but we didn't manage to discuss the spiritual leaders.'

The MP didn't follow up and Shaw continued.

'We will be moving our guests to more appropriate accommodation soon and no doubt there will be an opportunity for more discussion. This is a short statement. Now I'm open to questions.'

'Is he a good Socialist, Prime Minister?'

Laughter followed the likeable MP's question.

'Better than the Honourable Gentleman! No taxes are collected!'

'From the rich, you mean!'

'No, from anybody!'

'Well, if it helps the workers, I'm for it!'

'Good.'

'But where do they get the funds?' Another MP questioned.

'From the rental value.'

'Prime Minister, this is the land value theory. I've had certain people pestering me with this idea. It's primitive and impractical,' a further Member intervened with passion.

'Well the Honourable Member may wish to reflect how our visitors got here. That certainly wasn't primitive.'

'Freehold property is the foundation of the state!'

'Tell that to the young who can't afford a mortgage for a start-up home!'

That's another enemy he's made, the Chancellor thought, sitting gnome-like at the PM's side.

The Foreign Secretary sat forward on his bench and looked across: a well-groomed man, whose naturally cultured ways were perfect for his role.

'Prime Minister, did the Captain make any suggestions?'

'Venturing suggestions wasn't on his agenda, as it were. But he could answer questions. So I used an old political trick and asked him what he thought that I should ask!'

There were knowing smiles across the despatch box.

'And what did he say?' an opposition frontbencher asked.

'He was concerned at the erosion of core certainty, to use his words. It reminded me of Isaiah and I looked the passage up. This is it: *Truth is fallen in the street and equity cannot enter.* Your Prime Minister found it rather close to home.'

An agitated young man shot up on the opposite benches.

'This is Victorian pretension!'

'And what is your opinion? I must say, when it takes modern academics weeks to decide that a video-nasty is nasty, I sometimes wonder what has happened to our common sense!'

'Censorship's a fossil! It's dead!' The young MP shot up his hands in exasperation.

'Order! Order!' The Speaker's voice rang out. 'Will the Honourable Member control himself?'

The questions continued – curiosity questions in Shaw's opinion. Then, and with deliberate measure, the opposition leader rose and approached the despatch desk.

'May I congratulate the Right Honourable Gentleman on his handling of this momentous event. No one could have assured the nation better than he. There is nothing to fear and we can only wish our Visitors a happy sojourn with us. The Prime Minister has also suggested a prompt meeting with Her Majesty and this I support totally. And, Sir, may I thank you for quoting Isaiah. We need more of that.'

At that the opposition leader took his seat and the Prime Minster rose to thank him. He paused, amazed at his old antagonist's support, for it was real and from the heart. That was a most engaging thing about the House – when it was necessary, friendship and support often came from one's fiercest opponents.

'I am most grateful for the Right Honourable Gentleman's generous and substantial support. Indeed, at such a time as this we are one House, one Nation united in welcoming our Visitors from their distant planet.'

The Prime Minister sat down and the Speaker boomed the next business of the House.

After a brief word with the Chancellor, Shaw strolled out of the chamber with his friend the Foreign Secretary.

'Jim, I think you'd better meet these folk. After all, you *are* the Foreign Secretary!'

*

After the first undignified interviews with the Visitors, when they were accused of being frauds, Shaw determined to protect the nation's guests from further populist TV coverage. No doubt there'd be a hue and cry but the national interest – the dignity of the Nation – was in question. His press officer wanted all sorts of photo opportunities, but Shaw was quite determined that the first photographs released would feature Her Majesty. She was the Head of State.

He had procured an audience in the morning, when he would submit his proposals. In the meantime he would see the Visitors and discuss the detail and duration of their stay. Security, of course, was a major issue. There was always some sick soul anxious for the pale publicity of a headline.

*

Still slumped in his front bench seat, the Chancellor watched the PM leave the chamber. He was far from happy for in his eyes Shaw had acted like a stage-struck fool. He should have sent the Aliens packing! Instead, he'd fawned and grovelled. Well, Shaw would have to watch his back for there were many who were tired of his antics. Out of the corner of his eye he could see Samuel Burns slowly coming down the steps to the floor. Shaw had knocked him down and that was very foolish.

'Samuel,' he called, 'let's walk out together.'

'Ah, George...'

'Samuel, a few friends are gathering at Number Eleven tonight. Why not join us?

'Delighted, George.'

Chapter Four

Shaw assumed that the Visitors would visit other countries. So in his eyes every moment counted, before they powered off to the States or the East, or anywhere for that matter. He needed bright young men to follow up the Visitors' ideas, men strong enough to stand against the massed ranks of the vested interest. The Chancellor, that monument to fossilised ability, would do nothing, and the Education Minister was in the pocket of the academics. Dear God, he'd started off with all the usual good intentions. He'd picked the best men: another cabinet of 'all the talents'. They were the perfect team to set the nation back on course. Now, after barely a year, a major reshuffle seemed unavoidable. Indeed, with the advent of the Visitors, it was essential.

Toby Simpson...the name seemed to come from nowhere. Yes, he was the man, and if the press thought they had an easy prey, he'd soon relieve them of their misconception. The idea propelled him out of bed. A busy day lay ahead.

*

It had been a stimulating dinner party, with substantial conversation. No gossiping, thank God. The chateau-bottled flowed but it didn't seem to have the least effect. And that blonde angel that his sister had invited: she was special. A Classics graduate with a name to match: Drusilla, the feminine of Drusus. His schoolboy Latin still glimmered faintly. He yawned, stretched himself and checked the bedside clock again. It was almost 6 am. The phone rang. His hand stretched out sleepily.

'What is it this time?' he muttered. 'Yes, Prime Minister!'

Suddenly Toby Simpson was very much awake.

*

16

Toby Simpson, a crinkly-haired, trim-figured man above aver-age height, arrived at Number Ten at 9.30 as requested. Almost at once the Prime Minister greeted him.

'We'll talk in the car,' the PM said briefly.

Cromwell Road and the M4 approach were busy but not impossible. So, sandwiched between two blue-flashing police cars, they reached the M4 quickly. By then the PM had just finished scanning the newspapers. 'At times I do believe the public are informed by those who know the least! But there it is: part of our strange chaotic system that somehow seems to muddle through! Now, Toby...'

'Yes, Prime Minister?'

'I would like you to oversee our dealings with these far off friends. I don't want their ideas buried by the vested interests of some puffed-up minister's ego, or that of any pressure group or body. You will have Cabinet rank and you'll have my backing, provided you're not some retro-Leninist!'

'You haven't seen my tee shirt, Sir!'

'We'll get on well, Toby. This morning I'll be introducing you to "The Captain". He is a remarkable man ... being ... I'm not sure how to put it. His remit is to answer questions but not to initiate action. Seems a pretty non-aggressive stance. I trust them but, Toby, *be* your own man. It's the truth that matters not some hoary-headed vested interest.'

'On the economic front, the freehold vested interest will no doubt be the worst. We had the first shot in the Commons yesterday.'

'What are they afraid of? In the short term they wouldn't lose much. Even in the long term ... anyway, it would take years to implement. Too speedy a change would require a Stalin and you might be pleased to know that's not my style! And, Toby, I've got a feeling they'd be better off by far if this system were in place. For one thing, no death duties!'

'Have you any other thoughts or advice, Prime Minister?'

'Their views on education would be helpful. Some of our class-rooms seem to be unmanageable free-for-alls, and any hint of punishment sends the PC lobby into orbit. We need ideas! There are drugs of course, but they may not suffer from such self-destructive habits! Toby, the field's wide open.'

'You've given me quite a task, Prime Minister. Thanks for your trust.'

'Well, your name came into mind just as I was getting up. The gods directed, as it were! And, by the way, we'll be meeting Her Majesty this afternoon. Now, Toby, here's another issue. Whereas the Queen is greatly loved and much respected, the wreckers, though unintentional in the main, do not understand the benefits of our constitutional monarchy. I need ammunition to defend our priceless heritage. The Crown is the focus of excellence and the final guardian of our freedoms. It stands for the values of the spirit and represents humanity in affairs of state. Here is the final hope of mercy and a sympathetic ear. A faded politician tarnished by the hurly burly of political life cannot provide this. The monarchy is an awesome responsibility. If sometimes there are faults, we must remember the importance of the office. That we must protect.

'This tittle-tattle dominated media world makes the monarch's role extremely difficult. And here's another problem: what about the media's role? Toby, ask whatever comes to mind for we need the wisdom of these people. Indeed, I fear our nation has forgotten much about the richness of its heritage.'

Purring discreetly, the PM's Jaguar turned off the motorway at Junction 6 and headed for Windsor. Then, bypassing the town, it sped towards Winkfield. After a mile or so they slowed, turning into a rather unpretentious avenue. Once through a line of trees the scene changed dramatically. The Army were everywhere, and before them was a quite substantial mansion. The security check was brief, then on they went to park in front of the ornate entrance. HMG was doing the Visitors proud, Toby Simpson thought, but he made no comment.

Toby watched as the PM was warmly greeted by the Visitors' leader.

'I watched your report to the House of Commons. You were very complimentary, Prime Minister.'

'Deservedly so, Captain. Now may I introduce you to Mr Toby Simpson MP? He's one of the lucky ones who have a safe seat. Have I caught you?' Shaw smiled.

'Not this time. I understand the term.'

'Toby here has just been given special responsibility for your welfare and comfort. I can assure you that he'll ask you many questions, though none will cross the borderline of indiscretion.'

18

'I think by now tea will be ready. You were, of course, expected.'

Simpson was amazed at the urbanity. It was exactly as the PM described. His eyes, though, had a strangely placid quality. Indeed, all the Visitors shared this feature. Peace was a message not confined to words alone, it was in their very being.

Once in the inner hall, the PM suggested a meeting with the Queen.

'We would be greatly honoured,' the Captain responded.

'And a photograph perhaps, that would be given to the press?'

'We have no objections.'

✳

The Manor at Winkfield was three stories high, with a small-windowed pilot story at the top. It also had a basement, suitable mostly for storage. It was red brick, well matured with age, with a creeper scaling one of the corners. The garden was substantial but the walled enclosure had gone. Only the outer wall was left, against which a number of fruit trees were arranged. There were several stone-built office buildings – the gardeners and maintenance personnel used these – and there was also ample garage space. Yes, Toby thought, HMG had pushed the boat out.

Simpson had been allocated a small suite at the top of the house and there was an office for his secretary on the ground floor. Clearly it was a living-in job – but what a job! Toby knew he had been amazingly fortunate but, as the saying went, it wouldn't be all beer and skittles!

Chapter Five

Two days after the Prime Minister's first Commons report, a powerful article denouncing any proposal of 'an outdated and dangerous land levy' was published by a leading daily 'heavy'. Shaw had expected it the following day, but maybe that was being too cynical. The author, a leading professor of economics was a regular adviser to the Treasury and, as such, a frequent guest at the Chancellor's table. The professor's views would carry weight, and they were correct – but only if a substantial measure of the tax were instantly applied. No one was advocating anything so draconian and this was where the article was so frustratingly irresponsible.

That evening when he'd discussed rent-collection with the Captain over supper, he had been convinced of the efficacy of the measure. It was simply natural and beyond the realm of theory. The trouble was that the economy had become horrendously complicated and this had made application of the measure difficult. So the initial rental charge could only be a modest percentage.

The lead story in the papers was the environment. Here the door was being brutally slammed after years of neglect. In fact environmental concern was a ready tool for the envious in condemning the meanest luxury as extravagance. Of course, the horse had bolted years ago. What was the cause? As usual, experts jousted with the lances of their contrary opinions. In fact he had received the best advice from his own son. 'Dad, even if CO_2 is not the main culprit, it would do no harm to cut it back, just in case!' Shaw sighed. It was time for some Prime Ministerial statement, but what could he say other than the usual platitudes? Of course! The Visitors... maybe they had an angle! With luck Toby would already have asked them. He would deal with that tomorrow. Today was constituency day when he'd promised to meet the people at his 'Surgery'. He enjoyed that, but it didn't happen often nowadays, and anyway security spoiled it all. Being PM made sure of that.

✳

Toby Simpson had spoken to the Captain on the question of climate change, and his questions were answered without the least hesitation. The answers upended most of Toby's fixed assumptions, but he remembered learning about the American Indians as a boy, and how they viewed their land as sacred. The Captain took the same approach. Change would be a shallow thing which would not take root until the Earth was viewed with due respect.

Normally Simpson would have considered such comments naïve but, coming from such a remarkable being, he took them seriously. They had taken to having their conversations while strolling in the gardens, and during such times the Captain was forever admiring the amazing diversity of plants and insects.

'You live on a very beautiful planet, Toby,' the Captain had said. Simpson had suggested 'Toby' and the Captain had complied without a murmur. He, of course, was still 'the Captain'. Finally, after being silent for some time, he added, 'Reverence for Nature and the Earth are necessary. Without such reverence all your efforts will be weak and ineffectual for there'll be no heart in them.'

Toby could think of nothing more to say. It was ridiculous. Here he was with the most remarkable being he had ever met and he couldn't raise a question. Yet that busy creature in the mind would not give up. Round and round it went, searching every alley. It was a fruitless, tedious exercise and at last he gave it up and let the beauty of the sunny day bring peace.

The Captain seemed to be absorbing his surroundings like a lover. Heavens, it was peaceful. What a difference from the frantic life that seemed to be his lot. Westminster was such a hot-house with 'eager beavers' fighting for a foothold on the greasy pole. He was one of them, of course, one of the lucky ones – incredibly lucky, having landed a safe seat and a Cabinet post before the age of thirty-three.

The peace was still there, quietly fostering equanimity. At least ten minutes passed. Then a question came from nowhere, or so it seemed.

'How can we foster a sense of the sacred?'

21

'By praising the sacred,' the Captain returned without hesitation.

'I fear that I'd be laughed to scorn!'

'Knowing when to speak is "half the battle" – I think that illustrates my meaning. And always speak from stillness.'

Normally Toby would have taken such advice with the proverbial pinch of salt, but things were different in the Captain's company.

Simpson's mobile rang. He had forgotten to switch it to silent mode.

'Sorry, Captain,' he said, putting the tiny instrument to his ear.

'Yes, Prime Minister. I'd be delighted, Sir. Good bye.'

'The PM ...wants me to dine with him this evening.'

*

Nearing Heathrow on the M4, Toby's hands-off car-phone rang. It was one of the PM's secretaries.

'Mr Simpson, the PM asks if you have a lady you would like to bring this evening?'

'Kim, tell him that I'll scan my address book!'

The secretary chuckled and the phone went dead.

Suddenly his neat, organised world was shattered. His sister was always his safe bet but she was never free on a Wednesday. And the others? Nothing sparked. Then he remembered his sister's friend, the Classics graduate. He pulled on to the hard shoulder and punched in his sister's number, after which he was off again.

'Lizzie Simpson.'

'Lizzie, I'm assuming you're not free tonight.'

'Toby, you assume correct.'

'There's a dinner at Number Ten and the PM has asked if I would like to bring a friend, which translated means: arrive with a partner! What about your friend with the Roman name?'

'Drusilla? You'll be lucky, they're queuing up for her!'

'Well, sister, not every invitation is to dine at Number Ten.'

'Brother, that may enable you to swing it!'

He pulled over and took Drusilla's home and mobile numbers.

'Well, my lady with the Roman name: *jacta aleia est.* The die is cast.'

He punched the number.

Chapter Six

Drusilla Cavendish-Browne certainly had the name, but she also had the looks to match. What was more, her mind was needle sharp. Truth was, she frightened most men, especially those who felt they had to prove themselves. So, contrary to most opinion, she received few invitations and those she did she often felt quite painful for there was little that they shared in common except the physical, and that without sincere affection was, in plain terms, crude. Lizzie's brother Toby, though, was different. His mind ranged wide and the political realities he described were fascinating. So when she received his phone call she made no secret of her satisfaction.

He was handsome in a plain sort of way and had the kind of crinkly hair that would be unaffected in a gale. He was going grey but Lizzie had told her that her father had been grey at thirty.

The sheer relief of finding a partner for the evening was Toby's overriding emotion. But when he collected Drusilla at her flat he was stunned. What a beautiful and graceful person, he marvelled. And she was dressed so well, without the least concession to the scanty coverings worn by the fashionable. But then Lizzie's friends were mostly fairly civilised! He smiled. It was a good job the PC boys couldn't scan his thoughts!

*

The PM was at his fatherly best when greeting them at Number Ten.

'How graceful you look, my dear,' he said, gently patting Drusilla's hand. 'Toby, where did you find this beautiful lady?'

'My sister's friend, Prime Minister.'

'You have a powerful ally in your sister, it would seem!'

For Drusilla, the rest of the introductions, to Mrs Shaw, Sir James Huntington and his wife, all seemed to swim together in friendly confusion.

Pleasantries and banter eased the moments prior to dinner,

until unexpectedly the PM had a phone call. It had to be important, as he was not to be disturbed on such occasions.

'He never gets a moment to himself!' Mrs Shaw complained.

However, the PM was only briefly absent, but he clearly was annoyed.

'There's been an attempt to breach the outer ring at Winkfield. The press, of course, are sitting on the doorstep, so no doubt it will be all over the papers.'

'Who are the culprits, Sir?'

'The press will tell us in the morning!' Shaw returned cynically. 'There's more! Someone's had a scan of the early editions and apparently one of the chattering class heavies has run a cover story on the cost of housing and protecting our outer space Visitors. Can you think of anything so petty, crass and downright mean? They are our guests for heavens sake!'

'Don't let them spoil our dinner, dear!' Mrs Shaw said lightly.

Shaw laughed.

'Now you know the secret of my so-called unflappable image.'

The PM laughed again.

Drusilla was amazed, but gratified, for this was Downing Street, the Prime Minister was host, yet it was all so human, so ordinary. The conversation, though, wasn't ordinary and the PM's asides were the stuff of history. Toby held centre stage from time to time when he described his dealings with the Visitors. They all had two fields of expertise so they could double up, as it were, in times of illness. Their second-in-command was the medical man, but the Captain was also qualified. It was all fascinating and it was first-hand stuff. She was privileged and she knew it, but she also knew that she'd been checked out, as they said, for Toby had had to give Downing Street prior notice of her name and details.

'Why did they choose Britain?' She suddenly asked. Indeed it was her first question.

'Over to you, Toby,' the PM responded.

'Yes, I asked the same question a day or so ago. Apparently they started watching us quite some time ago, and I know they visited our island during the time of the Elder Pitt. Again they were present when the secret ballot was introduced, that is 1872, if my memory's right. The First World War greatly saddened them, for I think they'd become rather attached to our story.

24

They admire greatly our constitutional monarchy, but feel we don't appreciate our good fortune.'

Toby paused and looked round the table.

'They don't criticise, they don't make suggestions, but when we ask questions they answer and they give advice. Now, I really haven't answered Drusilla's question. Why are they not in America, or Russia, or the East for that matter? This was the nature of the question that I put. The Captain said we were a tolerant country and for many years a sanctuary of freedom. We were a lawful people and the level of corruption was still low. But we must be vigilant. We must not let our freedoms be corrupted by licence, and in our tolerance we must not give a home to arrogant intolerance. Here he was very strong indeed. We must defend our freedoms from the tyranny of equality groups and PC lobbies which often have the backing of the law.'

Again he paused but no one interrupted him.

'The US, Russia, China, India and the Islamic world they view as definite interest groups, whereas we, despite our links with Europe, retain a certain independence. In their opinion we are in some ways friends to all. So they see their stay on British soil as being neutral.'

'An interesting analysis, but I fear it would be judged a rather rosy picture: certainly by our friends across the channel who see us as a US poodle,' the PM said, smiling wryly.

'Prime Minister, I think we can expect requests from various governments for an audience with the Visitors,' the Foreign Secretary ventured.

'I sense a security nightmare and that would spoil the sweet. We're having a good old English pudding, you'll be pleased to hear.'

*

Mrs Shaw knew the signs. Her husband wanted some time with the men. So after the sweet she engineered a 'Cook's Tour' as she called it, which introduced Drusilla to the Downing Street warren, her pet name for the public rooms.

Once alone with the men, the PM listed his concerns.

'I'm pestered by the scientists demanding access to the Visitors. Those on the MOD payroll are the most persistent. The technical wizardry that the Visitors have would give our forces a massive advantage. This they stress repeatedly. Even the Defence Secretary is playing their tune. Have they never heard of the arms race? And if we had an advantage how long do they think we'd keep it? Sometimes I think the human race should be anaesthetised!'

Toby Simpson just managed to keep a straight face.

'Sir, I think the Visitors are well able to look after themselves.'

'That's my hope too, but you'd better confirm it and also warn them of the dangers. Where's their spacecraft?'

Toby pointed upwards.

'It's quietly orbiting. They can land it any time they want. To them it's train-set stuff!'

The PM nodded, looking across at the Foreign Secretary.

'What do you think, Jim?'

'Well, PM, I hate to say it, but I hope their stay is short!'

'Why, Jim?'

'I don't fear them. The human lust for power is what I fear. The prize is glittering and there'll be many overwhelmed by desire. I would substantially upgrade security.'

'Toby?' the PM prompted, expecting a response.

'I'll speak to the Captain. I think it best to tell him of our fears.'

'Agreed,' Shaw replied briefly.

Just then the phone rang.

'That'll be Winkfield, I suspect,' Shaw said, picking up the phone.

'Yes put him on ... Thanks for getting back, Brigadier ... you disarmed him? ... I see, they did ... remarkable ... yes I agree, quite remarkable ... Tell the press that Mr Simpson will make a statement in the morning and thanks again for keeping me informed. Sorry, Toby!' The PM smiled knowingly as he replaced the phone. 'Apparently some nutter, recently resident at one of Her Majesty's prisons, slipped through the Army's ring of guards but was immobilised by one of the Visitors. Apparently the nutter aimed to purge the world of the alien devils! Alas, not unfamiliar rhetoric.'

'PM, tomorrow I have a list of ambassadors to see. The dignity and prestige of the major nations demand access, and all want to be first!'

'Well, the US should be first and Russia next, after that the FO can do their diplomatic best. They're rather good at that.'

'The anti-US lobby wont like that!'

26

'That is boringly predictable. Jim, just make it clear that nobody dictates, except the wishes of the Visitors and those of HMG. And, Jim, you really ought to visit Winkfield – indeed tomorrow if you can.'

'It would need to be very early!'

'The Captain's always out and about well before six: there would be no problem. Oh, Prime Minister, would it be appropriate for Drusilla and my sister to meet the Captain? Their views would be interesting and, of course, they wouldn't be running to the press!'

'An excellent idea! Ladies can be very perceptive. Now, gentlemen, we have a busy day tomorrow so after tea and coffee we ought to shut the shop. I can hear my wife, which means the ladies are returning right on cue. My wife is rather good at these diplomatic interludes!' He chuckled lightly.

Chapter Seven

It was late spring and the Winkfield morning air was fresh. The sky was cloudless and the Sun was warm. The weather was perfect.

'What a beautiful morning, Captain,' Simpson called out when the leader of the Visitors drew close.

'Wonderful, Toby! I've just walked round the grounds and I must reiterate my thanks to your government. This is a most delightful setting.'

Even after two days of close contact, Toby found the Visitors' fluency amazing. Sir James though, was flabbergasted.

'Captain, meet Sir James Huntington, our Foreign Secretary.' The handshakes were firm and warm.

'The staff have prepared some refreshments. They'll expect us to appear, so we had best go inside.' The Visitors' leader smiled in an urbane, knowing way. Huntington could hardly believe it.

After refreshments they got down to business, but for the Visitor there was no change in the mode of his behaviour. Huntington was fascinated. The Visitor was behaving in the manner of a Himalayan guru who never seemed to be without a certain sense of presence. He had read about such beings often but here was evidence before his eyes.

'Sir, have you read much concerning the sages of that populous country, India?'

'You question well, Sir James, for their wisdom is profound.'

'Would you be interested if I sent some of my book collection?'

'Most interested!'

'I'm sorry to change the subject but there are certain practical matters concerning those who are clamouring to see you. Later today I shall be meeting the United States Ambassador, followed closely by the Russian and then the Chinese and Japanese Ambassadors. All want to see you, Sir, and all believe they should be first, or at least amongst the first! The question is, do you want to see them and, if so, how many in one day?'

'If they want to see me, I will meet them. The rest I leave to you.'

'The Prime Minister I know is anxious that you should not *in any way* be treated as a fairground curiosity!'

The Captain glanced at Simpson.

'That's another one!' Toby chuckled. 'The PM means a circus attraction, Sir.'

The Visitor laughed.

'The Prime Minister's concern is much appreciated, but we will leave the matter entirely to you.'

'You may receive rather pressing invitations, Captain,' Huntington emphasised.

'I understand, Sir James. However, with your permission we would prefer to remain in this idyllic setting. By visiting one we would need to visit the other, and so on. By "staying put", as you would say, we will avoid too pointed an offence. You have a phrase for it: "damage limitation"!'

Toby Simpson burst out laughing and Huntington was quick to follow.

'Captain, we're looking for skills like yours at the Foreign Office!' Sir James reacted and they laughed again.

'I feel the Captain would find it rather far to commute to the office!' Toby interjected.

Laughter again erupted.

'Sir, your skills are awesome and yesterday you amply demonstrated this when you immobilised the deranged intruder.' Toby looked straight at the Visitor before continuing. 'Yet we must be cautious, for there may be forces willing to sacrifice many lives to gain some access to your knowledge. Kidnap cannot be dismissed! I'm afraid the Army presence will be much more obvious as we're increasing numbers.'

'We have the ability to detect negative forces even at a distance. This is useful but we would be foolish to claim invulnerability.'

'That's another job for you, Captain: security at Windsor!' Sir James quipped.

'On Her Majesty's staff – that would be an honour!' The Visitor smiled broadly. 'Sir James, if I apply your well known law of supply and demand, I should be pressing for a rise in salary!'

With the humour there arose a genuine affection, indeed a tangible unity.

'Captain, how do you view the institution of the Monarchy?' Toby questioned. 'It's something I've been meaning to ask you for some time.'

'With great respect, for the Monarchy stands for the unchanging, and just as the universal Spirit cares for all so the Monarch loves and cares for all the subjects of the realm. The role of Monarch is a service and, being sovereign, personal aggrandisement is irrelevant.'

'I agree, Captain, but many would say that the Monarchy is hopelessly out of date and, what's more, undemocratic. Again, the spiritual dimension would be treated with derision.'

'To ignore the spiritual is to ignore the wellspring of our very being. Such an attitude is unfortunate. Your fair-minded belief in democracy is commendable but democracy on its own leads to confusion and a kind of anarchy.

'The Monarchy, the judiciary and the spiritual leaders should be seen as the protectors of the people. This is the true function of aristocracy. The rich are merely rich, but, when they use their riches in the service of the state, then perhaps they could be named aristocrats!' The Captain's smile was almost mischievous.

'This conversation is so rich that I'm most reluctant to depart but duty calls, for I cannot keep the Ambassadors waiting. I will send those books of the Indian sages as promised.'

*

Simpson and the Captain walked with Huntington to his car and then proceeded round the grounds.

'Captain, the media are strident in their accusations of a cover-up. The Government, they say, are working closely with the Aliens, but to what purpose? Nobody knows, they say. However "sources close to the government" are quoted daily. Who dreams up this fiction is a wonder. Again foreign governments maintain that we, the Brits, have cornered the knowledge for ourselves, and because of this the diplomatic knives are out. We thought we had laid all this to rest but we were naïve, for it's much too big a story. Every newspaper on the planet has it on its leader page. Have you any suggestions?'

'Toby, it is understandable that the nations are sceptical. They will find it difficult to believe that the technical knowledge needed for our journey and defence has not been acquired, at least in part, by you. We ourselves were surprised that you made no overtures. But, of course, we are forbidden to give away such secrets because of their military-use potential.

'Your press is full of speculation on the manner of our travel and arms technology, but your honourable Prime Minister made no mention of it, none at all!'

'He has no wish to initiate an arms race, for that is what he feels would happen. Anyway, he didn't think you would be foolish enough to pass your knowledge over,' Toby explained.

'And he is right; even so he has resisted obvious temptations for we are lodgers, as you say, and are imposing on your hospitality. Some gift or token in acknowledgement of your kindness is properly due.'

'I'm sure the PM would accept a box of chocolates!'

The Captain exploded with laughter.

'Humour is so honest and refreshing. Toby, perhaps it's time for another TV appearance. Maybe I can explain myself better and calm this endless speculation.'

'It might take the kettle off the boil, but I fear that speculation will continue.'

'"Kettle off the boil"? – Yes, I get it! Very good.'

Chapter Eight

The Prime Minister was weary and, unusually for him, irritable. What head of state hadn't phoned him? He hated platitudes, yet he had become an expert, serving them in dripping spoonfuls. Even so, it mattered little what he said, for few believed him. One Eastern leader plainly told him he was lying. The US President believed him, though, but then he was a personal friend. Australia, Canada and New Zealand simply assumed his statements to be true, but very few gave him the benefit of the doubt. His European partners mostly saw 'perfidious Albion'. Indeed, the majority of nations, with the possible exception of India, felt that England was up to her old tricks!

From the beginning Shaw had wanted to protect the Aliens from the free-for-all of a press conference, but Toby Simpson had persuaded him, saying it would demonstrate transparency. The Captain, Simpson maintained, could easily cope with any question that was thrown at him. Shaw still had misgivings, but the decision had been made and the setting chosen: the medieval splendour of Westminster Hall.

The broadcast was set for eight in the evening and, as adequate notice was given, the world press were there in force. Security was tight and evident, and for at least an hour before the broadcast experts had been discussing the various questions that were likely to be raised; but to the discerning viewer it was clearly fill-in stuff to set the scene.

Exactly on time, the Prime Minster and Toby Simpson escorted the Captain and his Deputy on to the platform. The buzz in the hall suddenly died. The cameras were live and the Prime Minister rose to speak.

'Ladies and gentlemen of the press, Her Majesty's Government have been careful of the dignity and well-being of our Visitors; indeed we view them as friends. Even though awed by their abilities, we have not pursued their secrets in a tedious way. They in turn have tendered no demands. They do not presume to teach or preach, but when asked they answer questions. Now over to you.'

'Ed Sloane of *The Washington Post*. Sirs, we have travelled with some difficulty to our moon, but your journey makes us look like toddlers at play-school. Can you give us some explanation regarding your means of travel?'

The PM looked at the Captain, who nodded, indicating that he understood the question.

'We are not permitted to share our technical secrets. Our Elders feel that such a sharing would be irresponsible as these secrets could be used for military purposes. You might call this patronising – I think that's the word. We, of course, see it as practical.'

'You are impeding progress, Sir!' A voice shouted from the body of the press.

'When progress means annihilation, can we call it progress?' the Captain shot back.

'Are you're telling us we can't be trusted?'

'That seems to be your view.' The reply was immediate but without the slightest rancour.

Yes, Toby mused, the Captain was coping very well. Toby knew the journalist, a bright spark from one of the 'thinking' papers.

'Thank you, Sir,' the journalist returned, acknowledging the honesty of the exchange. A nice touch, Toby thought.

Toby recognised a popular Australian reporter amongst the sea of hands and sure enough the PM picked him out.

'What do you think of us, Sir? And why did you choose the Poms?'

'"Poms"? I believe you call that a term of endearment?'

'Yeah, some blokes do!'

The Captain laughed. He seemed so much at ease.

'We admire your scholars and your wise men,' he continued. 'In what you call the East the Brahmins of India have fathered much wisdom. And here in the West you have the Egyptians, Socrates, and then Boethius at the time of Justinian, and closer to this time the Florentine Renaissance with Marsilio Ficino. There are the saintly men like Francis of Assisi and, of course, the Sufi saints and the Toaist masters of China. I hope that answers your question.'

33

'Captain, you're away ahead of me,' the reporter quipped and laughter rippled round the hall.

'Your second question: we chose Britain for we liked its independence,' the Visitor explained.

There was a roar of derisory laughter, especially from the Continental press, sitting bunched together.

'You choose America's poodle, Captain,' one shouted.

The Captain turned to Shaw.

'"Poodle"?'

'A pet dog, Captain.'

'Well, Sir, if the UK were a nation on our planet we would be happy to enlist the poodle's help!'

'It looks as if you're Britain's poodle!' someone interjected.

Shaw thundered into the microphone.

'Order! Ladies and gentlemen, this isn't a dog show; please act with some decorum.'

The sea of hands shot up again and the PM pointed.

'Despite your assurances, many of us believe your stay here is preliminary and that you'll return with overwhelming forces. Why come here at all, other than to gain eventual dominion?'

'Such motives don't excite our thinking,' the Captain returned. 'We neither have the will nor need to colonise. Similar questions have been asked before. Be assured, our Elders did impose strict rules of conduct. We are allowed to study political and philosophic thinking and observe the behavioural patterns. Aggressive acts are strictly forbidden.'

'Thank you, Sir,' the questioner replied. Toby noted he was with the German group.

The PM picked another raised hand from the forest.

'May I welcome you on behalf of the people of France.' The accent was marked and Toby wondered whether the Captain would need help. 'You mention Elders: is your system tribal based?'

'No, not in a mode that you would recognise. Our leaders are all mature men who have served the community justly and wisely over an extended period. They are selected by the Elders, who are assisted by a broadly based panel democratically elected from a body which is itself elected by popular vote. But those who vote must pass an oral test on statecraft. Taking the test, I might add, is compulsory.'

34

'Your system seems very authoritarian,' the questioner reacted.

'Wisdom is the authority, and our final arbiter is the Chief Elder. He is not elected but chosen by the previous Chief Elder. This post has been known to lapse as no one could be found who had reached a sufficient level of humility.'

For a moment there was silence. It was as if the whole body of the assembled press had been shocked into wakefulness. Toby watched the scene, fascinated, while wondering who would speak and how they would react. Would they see the Visitor as someone totally naïve or would they wonder at a people who'd evolved such rules.

Suddenly a hand shot up, followed by an avalanche of others hoping to be called. The PM picked the first: a New Zealand reporter Simpson had met when briefly visiting that country.

'Sir, humility is not the first word that comes to mind when reviewing our political leaders. Are we capable of following a system such as yours?'

'Modes of government should be fashioned according to the nature of their citizens. So what suits my country may not suit yours. There are common principles, however.'

'May we press for your opinion on such principles.'

At last someone was behaving like a gentleman, Toby thought.

'The laws both civil and economic should be made to serve the citizens and not oppress them. They should be simple and easily understood. We have always found that complication is the road to error.'

The New Zealand reporter took his seat, knowing there were many more clamouring to be heard. The Captain, though, did not let the matter rest.

'If you wish to follow up this matter I would be pleased to meet you at a more convenient time!'

'Thank you, Sir, I will!'

Toby Simpson winced, they'd all be queuing up!

Another raised hand had caught the PM's attention.

'Sir, what is your religion? From the description of your Chief Elder, he seems to be of the "meek shall inherit the earth" type.' The speaker was disdainful and his heavily accented voice did not disguise this.

'The meek do inherit the earth, and to confuse humility with weakness is to miss the point. Only he who has purged the hardness of ego can hear the commands of the spirit, and those commands take courage to fulfil.'

'You're a fraud. You're much too smooth and fluent. It's the English – they've always deceived us!' At that the agitated middle-eastern pressman jumped up and made for the platform. Then he stopped, frozen in mid movement, just like a statue. Westminster Hall was eerily silent as all were captured by the drama.

The Captain whispered to Simpson, who immediately spoke into his lapel microphone, and the security men already rushing to the scene began to move with care. First they removed the pressman's coat and shoes, then they practically did a strip-search, with a modesty ring of security men blocking the scene. By the time they had finished Toby received a call that the contents of the man's coat had contained an elaborate cigarette case, beautifully made but lethal. How he'd slipped it through security in the first place was a mystery.

Once the pressman was presentable, the Captain released his control and the man suddenly went berserk, calling for the vengeance of his God. Then he was led screaming from the hall.

Toby Simpson was very much aware that the Deputy had remained totally passive throughout. Such self-control was rare and Simpson was quite certain that the Captain's number two could have acted in the same dramatic manner as his senior in command.

The PM apologised to the conference for the interruption, saying in his best unflappable manner the predictable words that the troubled reporter would be 'helping the police with their enquiries'. And so the meeting continued.

A myriad of hands stretched for attention and the PM picked a well-known and respected London journalist. No doubt Bob Shaw was hoping for a stabilising voice.

'What we've just witnessed was little less than a miracle. You may well have prevented a tragedy, and for that we must be more than grateful. But, Sir, are we allowed to ask how you did it?'

'We have a facility for detecting dark intent. Also, some of us can thwart such troubled beings. However, I regret that I am forbidden to pass this knowledge on. As you can imagine, such knowledge in the hands of the unscrupulous would be disastrous. Here I would like to thank Her Majesty's Government, for not once have they pressured me or even asked me to reveal our secrets.'

Toby Simpson was once more amazed. The Captain was so articulate, so Oxbridge, as it were. It was little wonder that people were suspicious.

The London reporter was still standing and his next comment echoed Simpson's thoughts.

'I heard you speak on TV, Sir, yet I'm still amazed at your fluency. How is it possible, Sir?'

'Our people have an ease of assimilation. Our facility to memorise is highly developed. We, of course, take it for granted, just in the same way you accept the computer's ability to store large amounts of data. The mind, however, has much more capacity than normally imagined and on our planet this has been developed. I am blessed with this facility. I also studied this country at an equivalent of your university level. So, Sir, my ability is not an instant skill. Mr Simpson here tries to catch me out and occasionally he wins.'

'Very occasionally!' Toby responded and the Captain laughed lightly.

The questions continued and the Captain fielded all with ease but the Prime Minister sensed that the Visitor had grown tired. The energy used to block the troubled fundamentalist was probably substantial.

'Ladies and gentlemen, two more questions,' he said firmly.

'Sir...' someone immediately responded. Toby recognised the Iranian reporter. They had once met and he had found him most reasonable.

'It's been a privilege listening to you, Sir. Can I ask you about your planet's religious customs?'

'Our modes of worship accord more with your classical ancestors. We treat the forces of Nature as sacred. The great elements, our sun, our moons and sister planets we see as deities. Again like your ancients, we hold philosophy in high esteem and for this we owe you much. Your scriptures are full of wisdom. Indeed it is the main reason why we have returned again and again. But this is the first time we have revealed ourselves.'

'Why now, Sir?'

'Our Elders felt it was the time to give and indeed to share our common aspirations, for there is only one Supreme Good. That is what your Plato would have said.'

'I am honoured to have spoken to you, Sir.'

Another question could spoil everything, especially as he sensed a seething opposition, even rage. He was too late.

'I don't believe any of this cant. I hate it. It's stage-managed. I mean really – and the hypnotist's trick: that's simple stuff to some!'

'Good. You've had your say,' Shaw said angrily.

'No, he hasn't, let him speak!' Another voice spoke up, its author well hidden.

'This is a formal meeting, not a bear garden,' the Prime Minister growled. 'I don't know who you are or why you've come, but there's one thing that *we're* not here to do and that is listen to bigotry, whether it be secular, religious or political.'

Shaw caught the eye of a journalist he respected and the popular reporter took the hint.

'I do believe I have the last question. A privilege indeed. Sir, you have observed our ways, both good and not so good. What is your advice? How best should we conduct our affairs and in what areas should we amend our ways?'

'These are large questions, but there is one truth that transcends all. Your great teacher Plato said it; your scriptures repeatedly say it and we on our planet always try to follow their advice. That is, we should remember the Supreme at the beginning of every action. This is the first requirement of humility. Indeed it is fundamental for by falling still we start from stillness and not the swirl of busy action.'

Shaw smiled to himself, thinking that by now the 'God is dead brigade' would have blown their fuse.

'I am always loath to give advice as such for it seems to be self-righteous and presumptuous, yet you have asked the question. Civil law in this country is fundamentally natural and reasonable. The duties not to slander, not to injure and not to imprison without due process are understood by all as natural, but when it comes to economics the simple rule of natural law has been forgotten. To put it bluntly, it is not natural for the element land to be claimed by the few to the detriment of the many. The law of equity pertaining to the God-given elements is fundamental and it should not be ignored. On our planet location value is collected by the community, for it is the community which creates it, but when this value is claimed by private interests, as seems to be the custom here, poverty is rampant. In a nation where civil law and economic law are natural, men will be free, for what is produced by honest labour is untaxed and what is produced by the community's collective presence is collected by its creator, the community. Here we have the natural fund for all community services.

'You have banished civil slavery. What then of economic slavery? The creator intended no deprivation but mankind has created its own prisons by ignoring natural law. Discover the natural law and obey it! This is the answer to the problem of poverty.'

Toby Simpson had never heard the Captain speak so forcefully, but would the nations heed the message? For vested interest was entrenched not only in the mansion but also in the cottage. Freehold ownership had been encouraged for the thrifty and responsible, reasonable on the face of it. It was the greatest happiness for the greatest number, but happiness was not designed to be restricted. It was meant for all.

The Prime Minister was content. This was the moment to bring the meeting to a close. One thing was certain, the papers would be interesting in the morning.

＊

The Chancellor had booked a private room at his club and after the press conference, at which he'd been a guest, he and a number of his close associates gathered for dinner. A general mood of cynicism dominated the conversation. Apart from the Chancellor himself, four backbenchers, the Education Minister and a prominent economist were present. It was an influential gathering.

The Chancellor said little until the waitresses left after serving the main course. Then he kept his comments on the jocular side, saying that he hoped to take up hypnotism and add the practice to his party tricks. It was his economist friend who held the table's attention with his quips about the Alien's 'new age' economics. It was all very congenial, with no open criticism of the Premier. That moment was approaching, the Chancellor mused. Tonight was simply building up support, but he needed more 'big hitters'. The Chancellor had no doubt. He knew his time would come.

Chapter Nine

The papers were interesting in that the radical press were scathing and the reactionary elements were positive. Shaw had expected the conservative element to rant against rent levies but this had not happened. Indeed, one focused on the belief that death duties would be abolished. The radicals, on the other hand, were so wedded to their neo-socialist theories that they couldn't, or perhaps wouldn't, contemplate another way.

The following evening the media fielded the usual panel of experts. Shaw saw it as hopelessly biased, with only one journalist set against a TUC official and two established professors of economics. The TUC man said it was a charter to help the capitalist, and the professors were too busy defending their theories to give the proposals serious attention. The journalist, though, cut through the maze of complication, clearly rattling the university icons. One of them grew angry to the point of being inarticulate. No doubt the media bosses loved it, for it would justify repeats.

The next morning, that is two mornings after the press conference, the traditional papers carried the verdict of the well-known commentators. One dismissed the rent-collection measure with imperious disdain; two sat balanced squarely on the fence; but the panel journalist, who before had never been accepted, was given a prestigious column in one of the more successful 'heavies'. His reasoning was so self-evident that Simpson wondered how anyone could sidestep the issue. What was more, public opinion had clearly taken land reform to heart. This being so, politicians would be quick to follow, for votes were king!

The journalist, who had been immobilised by the Captain and held overnight by the police, was quietly put on the first plane to his homeland. Protests about his innocence were loud and full of outrage: a secret agent had planted the lethal cigarette case. It was the usual British trickery, they maintained.

*

The churches were now pressing for a joint meeting with the Visitor and it fell to Toby to arrange the venue and the list of invitations. This was sensitive ground and a task that Toby didn't relish. They were a careful lot: much of this was understandable as it seemed their various flocks were watching for the smallest slight.

Simpson was careful to keep the occasion as informal as possible. All would be seated in a semi-circle with himself, the Captain and his Deputy as part of the arc. Toby had decided to chair the meeting as the PM wanted to remain apart. The venue was the theatre in the basement of the British Museum, which was large enough yet not too large. The audience were by invitation only, but even then security was extremely tight.

The event was in two weeks' time, but it soon passed. Toby decided to invite his sister and Drusilla. Here was a chance to meet 'the angel with the Roman name', his private alias for Lizzie's charming friend. They would meet the Captain and his Deputy. He would see to that.

When considering who to ask, the civil service advisors had presented Simpson with a nightmare. Even the seating plan was controversial. The number of followers, however, was the most objective measure and this Simpson adhered to faithfully.

The media, of course, were building the meeting up, indeed stoking confrontation. It wasn't malicious, but rather an habitual pattern. The fraud theory was given generous air time, such was their democratic approach. Some religious leaders were vehement in their denunciations. Simpson felt their passion reflected, with some accuracy, their insecurity, for exclusive religion was most uncomfortable with what was, in factual terms, a universal view. 'Was the unending Universe to be condemned as heathen or infidel?' one amused commentator penned mischievously.

The media had never had it so good. The viewing numbers were astronomic and selling rights was child's play. Toby Simpson, whether he liked it or not, was a household name, not just in Britain but worldwide. His flat had a twenty-four-hour guard and his car always had an escort. Toby didn't like it. He had lost his happy anonymity. How could he ask Drusilla out, with a camera watching every mouthful?

*

The smallish theatre was full to capacity. The religious leaders had taken their places. At last the moment had arrived. Toby breathed deeply to calm his nervousness before walking out on to the platform, flanked by the Captain and his Deputy. They took their seats, that were to one side of the stage. (The planners had insisted that it was the better scheme.)

'Reverend Sirs, my Lords, Ladies and Gentlemen, it is the Captain's custom to begin each activity by remembering the Supreme. This I will leave to each of you to follow according to your tradition.'

Toby could see that one flint-faced fanatic was anything but happy, but at least he had the common sense to keep his mouth shut.

'With the near continuous publicity that follows their movements, the Captain and his Deputy need no introduction, yet we would be lacking in basic courtesy if we did not acknowledge the privilege of their presence, and that they have come a long way.' Simpson smiled. 'After all, their planet isn't exactly on the Piccadilly Line.' There was a brief burst of laughter. 'Panel, questions are welcome and expected so, without further ado, over to you!'

The Archbishop of Canterbury was the first to speak.

'Sirs, have you had great beings such as Christ and Krishna appear on you planet?'

'Not as such, and that is why we are attracted to your Earth, but some of our Chief Elders have been teachers of awe-inspiring insight. These sages are revered just as you revere the Buddha or the Prophet of Islam and the Lord Krishna or Christ.'

'Is the message of your sages similar, say, to that of Christ?' the Archbishop continued.

'"Blessed are the poor in spirit" – that is, blessed are those who lay no claim to spiritual riches. Yes, our Elders live by such humility, or at least they strive towards such wisdom.'

'Thank you, Captain. Yours is the answer of wisdom. It is as I expected. I am honoured.'

The Cardinal Archbishop was the next to pose a question.

'Captain, what of the Church and how is it organised?'

'We have temples, where we gather to hear the wisdom of the wise and where we contemplate the Supreme. Here children learn the moral codes and to respect their elders. There are ceremonies for the entrance into marriage and for other stages in the life. Prayer and meditation feature strongly, especially at those propitious times of dawn and dusk. Indeed there are many similarities with your churches.'

'Do you have a creed?'

'Those outstanding Elders of our past: their words are our creed.'

'What happens to those who leave the temple?'

'We can't leave what we never joined. The temple is the central pivot of the community. There is no coercion and therefore no desertion, but it would be very foolish not to go. There are those, of course, who join special groups. They may fall away but they never leave the temple, for that is their lifeline, their community and indeed their greater selves.'

'Thank you, noble Sir, you are most gracious.'

'Do you have statues and icons as a focus for worship?' an Eastern Orthodox priest questioned.

'There are statues fashioned with great devotion, and icons too, not unlike the ones you use. They can have great power depending on the devotion of the painter and the worshiper. Such a mode is natural for devotional people. On the other hand knowledge, that is knowledge experienced and revealed, is held in high regard. The Chief Elder always stresses the need for balance between the feeling and knowing aspects. I hope that answers your question?'

'My faith forbids the displaying of images, for the one true God has no image,' an Islamic cleric stated firmly.

'Yes, but how wonderfully you adorn your mosques with your flowing script. We once viewed your beautiful mosque at Isfahan.' The Captain smiled. 'We were "incognito" – I think that's the word.'

The cleric was a Shia, Toby noted. The Captain didn't miss a trick! Toby also noted that the cleric didn't smile, but this did not deter the Captain.

'Now to your question: if you've had a history where meaningless idols were worshiped, it is understandable that your leaders would restrain the habit. However I recall the words of an especially respected Elder who said that the surrounding creation was for the purpose of making the Supreme known. I think you will find this idea recorded in the Upanishads of the Brahmins of India. So, if art depicts a beautiful form lovingly dedicated to the Lord, it is also there for the purpose of reflecting the Supreme. Some find this idea useful, some don't, but either way it doesn't shake our firm belief in the Supreme, for which I believe your faith is also noted.'

The Captain had done his best to be respectful, but more importantly to speak the truth as he saw it. The cleric, though, stared at the floor, his piercing black eyes like lasers. His belief systems had been challenged and Toby could only hope that he could hold his volatile spirit in check.

Luckily another question was posed.

'Sir, what you say is challenging, but I strongly feel the need for certainty. Dogma is necessary: the people demand it.' The Cardinal had re-entered the discussion.

'Certainty yes, but not rigidity. On our planet there are two principles that we all adhere to, reverence for the Supreme and reverence for Nature. These we learn as children, along with the moral code. These are our certainties. No one questions them. It is simply how it is. For those who desire more there are groups of fellow seekers they can join. At festival times the proclamations of the Chief Elder are displayed for all to see. They are almost always of a spiritual nature. These rules and customs seem to suit the nature of our people. Even the disruptive elements mostly keep within certain limits of behaviour.'

'We're not the only ones who have disruptive elements then!' the Sunni Muslim cleric interjected, smiling widely. 'How do you cope with criminals?'

'A criminal is never allowed to walk free. Punishment protects the state and frees the criminal of his debt. There is another aspect though. Some young persons guilty of minor crimes are the victims of high spirits. We are a placid people, at times lacking the necessary fire that innovative thought requires, so we harness the penetrative energy of such high spirits. Indeed one such youth eventually became Chief Elder.'

'Thank you, Sir,' the cleric responded mildly. Toby knew him as a regular on TV panels. A safe bet, as it were.

'I like your emphasis on the moral codes and the idea of reverence for Nature. It seems infinitely reasonable to teach children in this way. Of course, the PC lobby would accuse us of indoctrinating the young.' The speaker was the Church of Scotland reprensitative.

'We have observed over the years how passionately you adhere to separate religious systems, and indoctrinating children has been, and still is in certain cases, a common feature. Now the pendulum has swung and it seems that you are, if I may use the phrase, throwing the baby out with the bathwater. The basic tenets of respect for the elderly, for father and mother, for your neighbour's property, and the basic prohibitions, not to steal, not to lie and so on, are hardly doctrinaire. However, while religions compete for ascendancy there will be problems. This wonderful diverse creation is the self-expression of the Supreme, so diversity is natural, but exclusivity leads to a separation, which contradicts the fact that creation is one and complete.'

'We are now used to your wonderful erudition, but I am still amazed and offer my congratulations. But, Sir, may I ask a further question?'

The Captain nodded.

'During the press conference at Westminster Hall you explained how ground rent was collected as the natural fund of the community. I rather feel that this is more a moral question than an economic one. What would be your view, Sir?'

'You're right, primarily it's a moral one, and only when it's seen as such will it be accepted. Is it moral for private interests to claim what the community has created collectively, and is it moral for the state to collect the private property of the individual? These are questions we should ask.'

The questions continued, with the Indian delegate answering one posed by the Captain relating to Vedic scripture. Toby's attention was still deflected by the Shia cleric, as from the time of his question he had remained staring in front of him, his eyes burning with the same fierce intensity. His hands were gripping his knees and Toby noted the whiteness of his knuckles. What inner tiger was he trying to contain?

The Chief Rabbi was now speaking. Toby had found him likable and easy in private; in public he understandably had an eye on his constituency. He was pursuing questions concerning the arts for which Jewish people seemed to have a propensity.

'The Elder whom I studied under was an artist and also a musician,' the Captain began. 'Time and time again he emphasised that great art brought the beholder or the listener to his inner well of peace. Indeed, we are very careful about the quality of music that's performed. The Elders watch this carefully and I believe the Ancient Greeks were similarly

45

watchful. Being too fussy is not useful, of course, but if some-one tramples down the gates of decency, we act.'

Once more Simpson was amazed by the Captain's skill with language.

'Thank you, may I ask another?'

The Captain glanced at Toby.

'There is still a generous amount of time,' Simpson said easily.

'Our laws go back to the days of the prophets; some obey them strictly and some not.' The Rabbi smiled. 'The Land we occupy is sacred to us and excites great passion. Is this something familiar on your planet?'

'Accepted custom has calmed such passion. But, as we said before, your fire and energy has produced great art. In other areas it will be equally creative, but measure is required, is indeed essential, for a talented and energetic people. I hope you don't think I'm venturing on presumption, but you asked a question!'

More thin ice negotiated safely, Toby thought, but his sense of calm was soon challenged when the previously benign countenance of the Sunni Muslim cleric suddenly exploded with outrage.

'Sacred land indeed! They stole *our* land!'

Toby knew he had to intervene, but what to say? He didn't have to, for the deep and authoritative voice of the Deputy boomed out, arresting all movement.

'The land is given; it belongs to no one. We are but brief custodians.'

Just before Toby sensed the babble beginning again, he called the meeting to a close.

'Reverend Sirs, my Lords, Ladies and Gentlemen: may I thank you all for coming, and especially thank the panel, most of all the Captain and his Deputy. This is indeed an evening to remember.'

Simpson's attention went immediately to the scene before him on the platform. The Buddhist cleric who hadn't spoken was escorting the Chief Rabbi to the Muslim cleric's side. There already was the fierce-eyed Shia, counselling calm. Then, by some miracle, hands stretched out and modest banter was exchanged. Only then did Toby search the audience for Lizzie and Drusilla.

Chapter Ten

The reception area was crowded and Toby Simpson noted that no one had left in a hurry, a positive sign in his opinion. The Shia cleric was talking animatedly to the Deputy and the Captain was continually engaged. Now, where were Lizzie and Drusilla? He scanned the gathering, seemingly in vain, then suddenly there they were, talking to the Archbishop of Canterbury. Who else?

'Where did you find these lovely ladies, your Grace?'

'Some secrets I guard closely, Toby! Very satisfactory evening.'

'No prizes for guessing tomorrow's favourite headline!' Simpson quipped.

'The land is given; it belongs to no one,' Drusilla quietly suggested.

'I said no prizes!'

'Toby, this location value would be very difficult to collect in today's conditions of sub-leases and tower blocks,' the Archbishop ventured. 'At least, that's what my advisers say!'

'Leaseholds and sub-leaseholds can complicate the issue, for as you know a long leaseholder may be benefiting from location value more than the actual landowner. The experts tell us that a simple transfer method can be implemented. However, the Captain keeps emphasising that the assessors must not forget the actual land location site, for the tax is on location advantage not on bricks and mortar. Sorry, ladies, for this complication.'

'No, no, I find the whole idea fascinating,' Drusilla countered. 'And, of course, there are articles in the papers daily – mostly listing difficulties, I'm afraid.'

'We're good at that!'

'I was mesmerised by the young Muslim cleric,' Lizzie said.

'So was I, Lizzie. I feel he was greatly affected by this whole event. Now listen, you two, I promised to introduce you to the Captain. You, of course, are welcome to join us, Sir.'

'Thank you, but I feel I'd better do a little diplomatic mixing!'

*

'Captain, meet Drusilla Cavendish-Browne and my sister Lizzie.'

'What gracious ladies,' he responded.

Drusilla was taken aback by the sheer Englishness of the Visitor's speech and manner. And those eyes ... their depth seemed fathomless.

'We are honoured to meet you, Sir.' The response was on her lips without apparent thinking.

'Sir, what roles have women on your planet?' Lizzie asked.

'Rather similar to here; indeed I often wonder at the many similarities. Perhaps we are a little more Victorian!' The Captain smiled. 'The lady is revered for she is the mother, the first teacher of the infant being. We have ladies who join what you call the caring professions and a few who join the guardian role of Elder. Ladies, of course, are valued for their insight. Some of the other nations on our planet are much more rigid in their rules and prohibitions but we have always held that self-rule is far superior to that which is imposed. That being said, freedom shouldn't be usurped by licence. I might add that self-rule is greatly aided when the laws accord with Nature and with reason.'

'Thank you, Sir,' Lizzie acknowledged, but she couldn't think of any follow-up. Her mind had gone completely blank.

'Have you discovered any other inhabited planets apart from Earth?' Drusilla questioned. The obvious question, Toby realised, that he hadn't asked.

'No, the conditions necessary for life forms such as us are narrow. But we've only scanned a little area. Space, as far as we're concerned, is unending.'

It was time to escort the Captain and his Deputy back to Winkfield. To take them to another dining venue was prohibited by security.

As usual there had been no time to have a private word with Drusilla. However, there was always the phone.

*

They were just about to leave when one of the security men rushed up with a mobile.

'Can't this wait?' Toby reacted with some impatience.

48

'It's the PM, Sir!'

'That's the answer – it can't wait!'

'Yes, PM.'

'I watched the TV coverage. It went well, with some rough weather near the harbour.'

'But it calmed unexpectedly.'

'Listen Toby – I'll not delay you for I'm told you're just about to leave. We've had a tip-off and, as they say, it's for real. Go directly to Winkfield and take the back route. Security knows. Don't delay in London. I'll ring about this later. Bye.'

Never a dull moment, Toby mused cynically.

✳

It was a fast trip and both the Captain and his Deputy clearly liked it. On reaching Windsor they took an unfamiliar road. Simpson had no idea where he was but the driver seemed *au fait* with every twist and turn. Eventually they reached the back entrance, which was hardly ever used except for farming needs.

They were barely through the door when the secure phone started ringing.

'The PM, I bet,' Simpson reacted. He was right.

'We got the bastards.'

'That was quick!'

'Blow-ins from the Hindu Kush. Our homegrown guys didn't like it! So the tip-off was fairly detailed.'

'Where did you pick them up?'

'They and some English-speaking aids were posing as workmen digging up the road. So we interrupted their labours!'

'God, a very British scene, just think…'

'Don't! Anyway Paddington Green is rather full tonight.'

'What sort of mind can justify this?'

'Fanatics justify whatever suits them. Toby, the security boys are worried about kidnap. Could you ask the Captain if he could neutralise a serious attempt?'

'Of course, Sir.'

'Enjoy your supper; we'll speak tomorrow, and give the Captain my good wishes.'

'With pleasure, Sir. Good night.'

Toby suddenly felt tired. It had been a demanding day.

Chapter Eleven

Supper was already prepared so they went to the dining room immediately. The other Visitors had already eaten and would join them later in the lounge. The Visitors were vegetarian and Toby fitted in with what was going. Anyway, he was halfway there himself.

'What was your general impression of the clerics?' Toby asked the Captain.

'They were polite and respectful and rather careful. After all, their respective flocks were watching.'

Toby nodded and turned to the Deputy.

'It seemed to me that some claimed God as their possession. The sound behind the words was eloquent,' the Deputy responded.

'Feels right. We're busy claiming everything else, why not God as well?' Simpson quipped. 'The PM sent his good wishes, but also voiced fears about your safety. Could you defend yourselves against a sustained kidnap attack – that is, one engineered by a large and ruthless foreign agency? Could you immobilise them?'

'No. That is the simple answer,' the Captain responded instantly. 'The energy required for one such incident, like Westminster Hall, is considerable. We are vulnerable to a sustained attack but we keep this to ourselves.'

'Would a foreign power make such an attack on British soil? Surely it would be a suicide mission, and most unlikely to succeed?' the Deputy asked.

'Covert forces backed by a powerful state who would, of course, disclaim responsibility... Your knowledge is the prize that glitters.'

'And we have put temptation in their way,' the Captain said quietly.

'That's no excuse for greed!'

'Even so, without our presence the problem would not have arisen. The Elders warned of this.'

'You must have other weapons?'

'To bring our craft to Earth would make the prize more obvious.'

'But can't you make it invisible?'

'When we came incognito, as it were, no one knew that we were present. Now they do. Invisibility in the current circumstances would be difficult. There is another problem. Our craft is well protected by repellent devices. These can be lethal to children and to many more, but we are forbidden to leave our vehicle vulnerable to damage or to those who wish to steal its secrets.'

'Catch 22', Toby reacted automatically.

'I read it,' the Captain responded on the instant.

'What haven't you read?'

All three burst out laughing.

'We'll probably have to move you to a more secure site, but not so attractive, I fear.'

*

As predicted, 'The land is given' was the front-page headline displayed by many of the dailies. Strangely the most conservative paper was the only one to add 'it belongs to no one'. Most, of course, concentrated on the Middle Eastern context and the wider meaning was ignored.

A call from the Downing Street press office alerted him to the first overt attack on the Captain, so he was prepared. It was one of the radicals. Why had the editor allowed it? Don't ask silly questions, Simpson! He began to read.

'How dare this Alien question our time-honoured customs that have delivered unprecedented wealth. This government should stop his endless pontificating and pack him off to his distant planet. We are quite capable of looking after our affairs. And as for the land levy, cranks have been peddling this simplistic theory for years. It may have been fit for the Middle Ages but not for our sophisticated society. Just take one look at a city tower block and ask the question: how would land tax be applied? Need I say more?'

'You arrogant bastard,' Toby muttered. Had no one ever told him how to treat a guest? 'Unprecedented wealth'! What about poverty? Had this closeted intellectual ever visited the umpteen hellholes round the country that were called estates? Who was

51

the guy anyway? Surprise, surprise: a leading member of a prestigious economic think tank. The Captain had trampled on his lovely theories and he didn't like it, not one little bit. Simpson chuckled and his anger cooled.

He sat back in his chair. The Utilitarians had a lot to answer for, he mused. 'The greatest happiness for the greatest number.' Sounds good, but tell it to the estates. Happiness is for all. The Captain had simply tried to point the way.

He stretched himself. Another car journey loomed – Downing Street for lunch.

*

The PM was in buoyant mood.

'I'm just like the US President: every day there are poll ratings, but today the news is good. I'm doing fine, they say. Do they think I'm some performing puppet?'

'Sir, you should enter the Eurovision Song Contest, it would do wonders for your image,' Simpson quipped.

Shaw laughed heartily.

'Now, this kidnap threat: what did the Captain have to say about his powers of immobilising assailants?'

'It uses too much energy. They can stop one but two would be difficult.'

'I see. Well, this must be kept strictly secret for it's a good deterrent!' He paused, bowing his head before continuing. 'The security boys are quite engaged, ground intelligence backed up by satellite point to special preparations in two large authoritarian countries. The exercises are being held close to submarine bases. Personally I think the SIS is being paranoid. They say that some of these Special Forces are so puffed up with pride they'd try anything.'

'The political leaders would never sanction such a thing!'

'Not officially, but I tell you one thing: they wouldn't say no to the goodies!'

'The whole thing sounds completely bonkers.'

'Yes, Toby, but I can't ignore the experts in a matter of defence. We'll move them to a military base. It'll not be so comfortable but there it is. Well, it's lunchtime. Let's have a bite and you can tell me all about the clerics. Canterbury was very gracious, I believe.'

'Yes, they all were in their special way.'

52

'This press thing...' the PM began as he entered the lift to take them to the flat. 'I tore a strip off the editor and he, of course, pressed the freedom of the press button. Anyway, our parting was friendly enough. I think you'll find that he'll accept a reply. You get my drift?'

'Loud and clear, Sir.'

'Welcome, Toby,' Mrs Shaw called out as they entered the flat. 'How is your sister and the lovely Drusilla? I saw them last night. The second row, I believe.'

'You're right. Yes, they're fine. I only see them at official functions at the moment.'

'Is that a complaint?' the PM joked.

'Nope, as they say in the Westerns.'

They took their seats.

'The Captain's shamed me into saying grace again. So may we be silent for a little while?'

'I was rather impressed by the young Shia cleric,' the PM started up almost immediately.

'So was I, Sir. I thought he was going to blow up, he looked so intense.'

'Yes, but then up he gets, comforts the elderly Sunni and amazingly calms him down. Human nature, human nature... if only we gave it a chance. Why are we so blind?'

'As they say, that's a good question.'

'Toby I'd like to meet that young man. You know, find out how he ticks.'

'That can be arranged.'

Chapter Twelve

Toby Simpson knew he needed expert help in countering the scathing article that had so annoyed him. His essay had to be convincing. Stating the principle was easy, but the 'tower block' question needed a substantial answer. A bland broad-brush response simply would not do, and in the circumstances would be irresponsible.

Now that he had a driver, an amazing but necessary perk, he could use the travelling time to phone. They had left Downing Street at two and by the time they'd reached the M4 Toby had tracked down an old school friend who knew about Site Value Rating and, over the years, had followed up with a degree at university. Tom Wynter was his name, a damn nice chap in Toby's estimation.

Simpson punched out the number just as the car entered the elevated section at Chiswick.

'Tom, it's Toby Simpson here.'

'Toby, what's a world celebrity doing phoning this non-entity? How are you, you old devil?'

'Bloody busy, Tom. I need your help.'

'I'm expensive!'

'I was afraid of that. Listen, did you read that article?'

'In the chattering class daily? Yeah – I'm still seething!'

'Can you counter the "tower block" question with convincing know-how?'

'Detailed studies have been made. First the chief beneficiary of the community-created value needs to be identified.'

'That's a bit of a mouthful, Tom!'

'Well, that's what we would be trying to collect, but only a small percentage at first. Let's call it CCV.'

'Sounds like a spy camera!'

'Toby, you were in PR too long! Now, the chief beneficiary in a tower block situation may have a long lease and may have a number of sub-lessees. They also may be benefiting from

CCV, though only marginally. So it is complicated, but by no means impossible.'

'But what about the freeholder?'

'They hold the sovereign base on which CCV is collected. No matter how complicated the situation this should never be forgotten, for eventually, when all the leases fall in, the freeholder becomes automatically the chief beneficiary of CCV. And Toby, long leases are not too common nowadays. But always, always the CCV is not a charge on bricks and mortar, it is on the site advantage of the land! This can be calculated, but we need a general valuation. Fortunately, with modern mapping and computer technology, this can be achieved quite quickly now.'

'Tom, just one point: it seems to me that the sub-lessees could have a rough deal, for they could be paying their rent as well as the CCV levy.'

'They can deduct the CCV levy from their rent to the main leaseholder. Toby, it's checks and balances; it's "easy peasy". Listen, feed all the info into a computer and the programme does for you.'

'For you guys it's always bloody easy, but for "thickos" like me it's a struggle! Tom, could you join me at Winkfield for an hour or two?'

'When?'

'Well today, but I know that's pushing it. The fact is I need to get this article to the paper fast. The bribe is you could meet the Captain!'

'All right, you've got me. But what about security?'

'Ring me when you pass Windsor and I'll wander down to the gate. Security is pretty fierce at present. Thanks, Tom.'

They exchanged mobile numbers and Toby sat back. He could see the Castle coming up on his left. The turn-off to Windsor would be soon.

*

Tom Wynter was on the phone within half an hour of Toby's arrival and Toby set out for the entrance.

'My God, Tom, you've grown a beard! Otherwise you haven't changed a bit.' Tom had 'a lean and hungry look' but could always be counted on.

'And you, well I see you on the box. You look so relaxed!

'Yes, like the ducks, paddling like hell underneath. Tom, thanks for such a prompt response. You must have dropped everything.'

'When you get a call like yours you'd be a fool to hang around! It's a fair step to the house – do you want a lift in my banger?'

'Tom, you'll have to leave it here. The rules are pretty strict – sorry!'

'Good God, security *is* tight!'

'Got yourself married yet?' Simpson asked as they set out.

'I'm betrothed, as they used to say in the distant past, and she doesn't seem to mind a pauper!'

'Come, Tom, everybody knows the Wynters are loaded!'

'Old money, Toby! The truth is we can't find a bloody house we can afford, and I can't move away from London. So we're trapped.'

Toby sensed the passion behind the words. How many couples round the country could tell a similar story? Countless, was the answer.

'Well, this is our great property owning democracy!'

'That's a misnomer! It's a land owning democracy. Buildings etc start deteriorating from the instant they're erected. It's the land, Toby. That's why the rich get richer and the poor never raise their heads!'

'What about negative equity?'

'That's the cruel dilemma that someone like me must face. Do we buy now or wait until there is a crash? And, if there were a crash, would I have a job?

'But the rich would take a hammering too!'

'Only if they're bloody fools – that is, greedy! The clever ones just wait, and when the prices reach their trough they snap up the bargains and wait until the market finds new life. You can't blame them, for our mad system allows it. The strange thing is that, when I explain this to a fellow sufferer, as it were, it doesn't seem to penetrate. A place on the ladder is the golden dream, but when they get the prize they're all too often ready for the box! Anyway, they probably think I'm some sort of fanatic, a kind of economic missionary.'

They walked on in silence. Tom was impressive; his words were punchy and arrested the attention. He certainly had the fire and he had the necessary academic background, but Simpson didn't want to 'wheel him out' too soon. But he'd have to decide within the next few days for the opposition were beginning to field their biggest economic guns. Tom, this could be your crowning moment. *Carpe diem!*

Tom's manner with the Captain was entirely appropriate. His questions were both penetrating and respectful and he also quickly matched the Captain's ready sense of humour. The lunch was long and leisurely and, after a brief walk in the park, Simpson and Wynter withdrew to craft the article to the radical daily.

Before they started, Tom Wynter sat back in his chair.

'Toby, I've been dedicated to this idea since I was a teenager, but until today I never really saw the question as a moral one. But it is; it *is* a moral question!'

Chapter Thirteen

After the reply to the article had been e-mailed to the paper and after Tom had headed for home, Toby felt that he deserved a nightcap with the Captain. Just then his mobile rang. It was the BBC pressing for a panel where experts from either side of the argument could battle toe to toe about the rights and wrongs of the issue.

'*Could we have the Captain? That would be fantastic if we could.*'

'No way, Tim, I'm not going to subject him to that bear garden.'

Tim was Tim Bates, a BBC producer that Toby had got to know over the past two years: a decent man, in his opinion, and one who didn't loose his sense of perspective.

'Who have you got?'

'*That guy who wrote the article for one of the radical heavies and a professor from Cambridge. They're queuing up! But I haven't got a soul from the pro-Captain lobby, if we may call it that. So I'm hoping you can help!*'

'Professors who are simply "sympathetic" with the idea, waffle. We need speakers who know their subject backwards. Yes, I think I can get two. Who's in the chair?'

'*Me! You may think it an ego trip, but the truth is I need someone who isn't a name that's going to upstage the lesser mortals!*'

'What's this, an outbreak of modesty?'

'*Realism! Toby, I've heard the Captain twice. I'm convinced!*'

'Well if you keep your nose clean I might get you a one-to-one. Mind you, it would have to be vetted.'

'*That would be quite a privilege. Thanks, Toby, and the vetting's OK. Now for being a good boy I can get you a special viewing box at the panel thing. One good turn deserves another!*'

'Tim, I can't be seen near the place! The cameras would be following me like a pack of wolves!'

'Don't worry, you'll be behind special glass where you can see out but no one can see in!'

'Yes I've seen that stuff on the movies. Thanks, Tim, I'll ring you tomorrow when I feel more *compos mentis*.'

Toby felt like stretching his legs out in one of the Captain's easy chairs but, just as he as he turned the handle to the drawing room, his mobile sprang again to life. It was the PM and he wasn't wasting words.

'We're moving them tomorrow. I don't like it, you don't like it, but the MOD is edgy. They want the security of a military base away from a civilian concentration. In fact, they're talking about a kidnap attempt as if it were a solid expectation.'

'Can I tell the Captain?'

'Yes, but tell him to keep it to himself. The staff could gossip down the pub!'

'My mind seems to be a total blank!'

'That's maybe just as well. I'll phone you in the morning. Apologise to the Captain and tell him I'll ring in the morning.'

'Thank you, Sir.'

Immediately the phone went dead.

Toby was very conscious of turning the brass handle of the Captain's drawing room. But the scene was so relaxed and peaceful that all his tensions vanished.

'Ah, Toby! You look as though you've had a busy day.'

'Not really, Captain, but I rather feel that I've been much too busy in the head!'

'Not so many realise that, Toby. Indeed, I think some call it being dynamic!'

They laughed, and Toby was reluctant to pass on the Premier's news.

'Many visitors today, Sir?'

'Just one. Sir James arrived with a rather pompous foreign minister who made no secret of his anti-British sentiment. So I told him that Great Britain had been most attentive to our needs.'

'I think, we're rather flattered that you chose us, Sir, but I'm afraid I've some rather inconvenient news. We're moving you to more secure premises. The PM is most apologetic and will phone you in the morning.'

The Chief Visitor smiled with what was clear amusement.

'Toby, you use such diplomatic language.' Then the Captain laughed. He seemed so totally content.

Toby said no more. What was the point? It was very clear that the Captain trusted HMG. It was flattering but quite a responsibility.

'How's the London Library coping with your requests?'

'With great efficiency. Couriers deliver daily. Your friend, the Secretary, is what I would call "one of the old school". I love your language, it's so pictorial.' This time the smile was even wider.

'Captain, I'd almost forgotten. Just a few moments ago I had a call from an old BBC acquaintance. He suggested an open forum, which I rejected, for I could only see a glorified squabble between large egos with little brain.'

'The "bear with little brain" – Winnie the Pooh!' the Captain returned at once.

Toby exploded with laughter.

'How do you do it?'

'I don't! The mind makes the connection!'

'Yes, but something nods!'

The Captain smiled, and Toby felt that he was close to tears. That hadn't happened before. He waited a moment before speaking.

'In place of an open forum, would you be happy with a one-to-one? This friend of mine isn't a name, as it were, but he's a decent man. I trust him.'

'Of course. Toby, you're very protective.'

'I'm careful of your dignity, Sir, and the dignity of our country. The PM is adamant that you should not be subject to shameless publicists, and they arrive in many forms! I'm glad about the one-to-one, for the media are pressing for more airtime. Your meeting with the President will be televised. He needs that for the folks back home, as he puts it. The President's a good man.'

'Toby, the President of who?'

'My heavens, I'd forgotten to tell you: the President of the United States. Air Force One will be here in the next few days. It hasn't been announced yet – the usual security high alert stuff. Captain, I would prefer that you kept this to yourself...'

The Captain burst out laughing.

'"I would prefer..." I'm sorry, Toby, but you are so very English – but please carry on.'

'Not until I've had a laugh myself!'

They both chuckled.

*

'Air Force One should be landing in the next few days. Apparently it's a flying visit but no doubt he'll have a session with the PM. They're pretty close.'

'An Honour indeed.'

'Yes Sir, the trouble is we'll probably have a rush of copycats.'

'I don't mind, Toby.'

'I know, Captain, but some of these state heads are not good company.'

'Then maybe I can aid their reformation!' The Captain's mischievous smile was obvious. 'Toby, do as you think best!'

'Thank you, Sir.'

'Toby, we've forgotten our traditional nightcap. Let me pour you one!'

'I thought you'd never ask!'

The Captain broke into easy laughter.

'I like that, Toby.'

Simpson watched as the Visitor from a very distant planet poured liqueur into two small glasses. The Captain's movements were seemingly effortless and, as he wore similar clothes, he could have passed for any 'Earthling'. It was the eyes, 'the windows to the soul' as they were once believed to be, that set him apart. Otherwise he could have been the man next door.

'Cheers!' The Visitor said, clinking Toby's glass.

They sat down.

'Toby, I would like to thank you for your kindness and indeed your friendship. I trust you, as I do your Prime Minister. This means a lot to me as I have the responsibility of ensuring the safety of nine souls. You have never asked awkward questions. You haven't even asked how long we're staying. There have been no complaints about costs, for the expenses must be high.'

'Some opposition MP brought this up in Parliament at Prime Minister's question time and the Prime Minister's answer was, to say the very least, abrupt. First, he reminded the House of hospitality and secondly he fired off statistics listing the sudden rise in tourist revenue. No one has brought the subject up since. So there you are, Sir, you're a revenue asset!'

'Clearly we will be going home but when is not completely in my hands.'

'Are you implying contact with your planet?'

'The laws that govern the mental world are of a different order from the physical.'

'My God, so it would appear!'

Chapter Fourteen

In the morning the MOD changed their mind. Whereas before theory had transcended common sense, now common sense had won. The Visitors were to stay at Winkfield and the Army were to double their defensive shield. Simpson had little doubt that the PM's strong objections had prevailed.

Toby was, to say the least, relieved, for the modest stately home at Winkfield was ideal, especially for the forthcoming visit of the US President. Indeed the backdrop of the Manor leant a dignity which reflected rightly the hospitality of HMG.

The phone had started ringing at 6.30, but Toby was already up and dressing. His small garret flat at the top of the big house contained a miniscule kitchen with a mini-fridge, a microwave and an electric kettle. He made himself a mug of tea and scrambled down the stairs to the office, fortified with the news that the Visitors would be staying put.

Tom Wynter was his first phone call.

'You're on, Tom, prime-time Thursday coming. It's the Question Time slot. And could you persuade that journalist friend of yours to join you. He's pretty good on his feet. Tim Bates is the BBC contact. Anyway, I'll send all these details by e-mail. And, Tom...'

'*Toby, this is big. God, I feel my knees knocking already!*'

'Tom, my knees still knock. You know your stuff. It's the wafflers who get into trouble. You'll be fine. Tim Bates has given us an incognito viewing room. Yours truly and a few other Wynter supporters will be there. Would Richard, that handsome brother of yours, like to come?'

'*I'll ask him. Toby, this scares hell out of me but thank you for the opportunity. At last we can tell the world the principles of economic justice. God, that sounds pompous!*'

'Never mind. Listen, I'd better send these details down the line. I'll speak later. And Tom, you'll be fine.'

The e-mails on Simpson's laptop seemed endless. Most were from the Foreign and Commonwealth Office giving prior warning of future callers on the Visitors. Sir James, it seemed, wanted to make a fuss over the visits of the Premiers of Australia, Canada and New Zealand. He was suggesting a joint meeting with the Queen, and the PM also in attendance. The Premiers could also have separate meetings. They were family, as it were, and we were justified in making a fuss. Sir James was, very much, one of the old school.

Toby also noted the imminent arrival of the French President. That would be another red carpet job, and a thick pile carpet too! He smiled. It was best to see the old rivalry as amusing. Taking it seriously had cost too many lives.

Out of the window he could see the Captain returning from his morning walk and at once he went out to meet him.

'Toby, what a beautiful morning – all given by the bounteous Supreme. All is his reflection and all reflects his unifying love.'

On the instant Toby's eyes were full and tears were very close. Embarrassed, he turned his head to the side. What's happening to me? His words were silent but intense, and as on the previous evening he waited for the embarrassment to pass.

'Sir, good news! We don't have to move after all. I think the PM put his foot down.'

'Very good, we find it quite idyllic here.'

'I'm afraid the military presence will be much more obvious.'

'Toby, to be restricted by security needs is understandable. You must do what you think is best.' The Captain smiled. 'In any case, we had a little look around before we showed ourselves!' The smile continued. 'Do you have to go into London today?'

'I'm afraid so, Sir. I have to make a statement to the House.'

'Do you find that difficult?'

'Let's say, you need to have your wits about you! Humour helps; if it didn't I fear my temper would be overstretched! The House can be a chastening experience. Ministers are servants, not masters!'

'We've always admired your parliamentary system. Have you time to join us for some breakfast?'

'I'll make time, Sir!'

*

The House of Commons was crowded, reflecting what was growing into an insatiable interest. A year ago such high-profile exposure would have exhilarated Toby, now that didn't seem to matter. Indeed, he wondered at his strange detachment as he waited for the Speaker's call.

Simpson scanned the packed benches opposite. What were they all thinking? What were their ruling attitudes? What did they really want to know? Who were these people? And who was he, for that matter? Snap out of it, Simpson, he grated, glancing at the Speaker, who as if on cue boomed out the preliminaries. Toby stood up, opening the folder that gave the detail of the Visitors' activity.

'Mr Speaker...' he began. It all felt so strangely dreamlike. Even so, he proceeded reporting on a businesslike list of meetings and callers at Winkfield, along with the immanent visits of the US and French Presidents. He also emphasised the undemanding and amenable behaviour of the Visitors. He did not wish, he said, to reveal security details other than to say it was currently being strengthened and was under constant review. He then resumed his seat and awaited questions.

The old familiar MP from the Midlands was the first to catch the Speaker's eye.

'Minister, do these friends of ours ever meet ordinary working folk? It seems to me that all they meet are toffs and diplomats!'

'Well, he meets me every day!' Toby smiled and was obliged with a ripple of laughter. 'Quite often I see our friends talking to the gardening and maintenance staff, and of course there are the soldiers, so it's not just diplomats, churchmen and politicians. Security fears, of course, restrict, which is a pity. As you know, we were lucky in foiling a murderous attempt. Why some people want to kill our Visitors is beyond my comprehension!

'You will appreciate that I cannot reveal all our security fears, other than to say that there are many curious minds who rather covet the special technical knowledge that the Visitors clearly have. As I've said before, our guests are forbidden to reveal their secrets as their Elders fear they'd be misused. And here, I'm sure, the Honourable Member would agree with the PM: we don't want another arms race!'

Toby briefly took his seat, and then rose again to answer the next question.

'Minister we've heard very little of how our guests conduct their lives on their own home planet, if I may use the term. How big are their cities? How are manufacturing enterprises run?

Do they share our obsession with growth and, if so, how do they dispose of the waste?'

'They send it here!' someone shouted and there was a burst of laughter.

'The Honourable Member has posed most interesting questions which I will follow up with the Captain and his friends. However, from the conversations I have had it seems certain that the manner of their manufacturing is wholly different from our methods, for the simple reason that they do not have a pool of people looking for a job as we would have. Because land is readily available on payment of a market rental, unemployment is minimal. So large enterprises appear to be free associations of the self-employed grouping to fulfil a need. Some of these entrepreneurial associations are semi-permanent. There are servants, of course, those not given to the organisational side, but they are not exploited; quite the contrary, as business leaders see them as a vital part of their concern. If they were exploited they would simply leave. On his planet, the Captain emphasised, shortage of labour always keeps the wages high. This may be difficult for us to understand but, where labour is untaxed and land is accessible for an annual rental, self-employment mushrooms and in the nature of things many need an extra pair of hands, if I may use the term. As for growth rates, I rather feel that this is foreign to their thinking. Indeed, the Captain asked me how we could sustain continuing growth rates in the long run on such a populous planet? Our throwaway society seems foreign to him. I shall ask about the waste disposal methods and inform you, Sir. Thank you for your question.'

'The Right Honourable Gentleman's answer is most interesting and deserves due study. Thank you, Minister.'

Immediately a well known and frequently cautioned MP from the North jumped to his feet, his passion leading him like a dog on a lead.

'I don't believe any of this claptrap. These guys speak too well. Everything is too good to be true. Where's their spacecraft, for heaven's sake? Circling the Earth, they say! Well, if you believe that one, you'd believe anything. This land guff is dreamland. Anyway, we're much too bloody selfish to put it into practice and...'

'Order! Order!' the Speaker thundered. 'If you persist in using unparliamentarily language you will be suspended!'

66

The young MP resumed his seat, glaring fixedly in front of him.

'The Honourable Member who has just spoken has made a telling point, for selfishness is a major problem. We all like pocketing the community-created value that accrues to our property simply by its position. One gentleman from Richmond told me that he made more money from the rising value of his property than from a lifetime's employment. Now, this is obviously and completely out of balance, yet we would find it difficult to surrender even a small percentage of this gain to the community which, as we've said, is its creator. So I'd like to throw our colleague's blunt assertion on the floor before us, as it were. Are we too selfish to put this measure into practice? That's a question for us all.'

Toby paused, and briefly there was silence.

'I have the privilege of meeting the Captain and his friends most days. In my mind there are no doubts. It's their eyes ... no, one could fake that ... Now, if the Honourable Gentleman still has doubts I am willing to introduce him to the Captain, even this afternoon, for I'll be driving back to Winkfield.'

The MP stood up and for a moment he remained with his head bowed.

'Mr Speaker, I apologise, my frustrations got the better of me; and yes, I will accept the Minister's offer. Thank you, Sir.'

'Mr Speaker, I am grateful to the Honourable Gentleman for his honesty which, I feel, has greatly helped to clear the air.'

After two more questions the allocated time was running out. Toby summed up briefly and then sat down to a friendly pat on his arm from the Foreign Secretary. The Chancellor, sitting on his other side, wasn't so forthcoming.

In the Lobby a porter handed him a phone. It was the PM.

That was good, Toby. The answers were good, and the drama. That clinched it, for people will remember. They always remember the drama!'

'Thanks, Prime Minister.'

The phone went dead. That was the PM. Wasting time was not his style.

Chapter Fifteen

The MPs name was Frederick Sharpe. Most called him Freddie and most, used to his fiery interjections, were not surprised at his latest performance in the House. He was likable, predictably wild, but very able. Few beat him in debate. His mop of hair was rarely combed, yet he always dressed respectably. Presently he was sitting in a ministerial car, the guest of Toby Simpson and not a little bemused at the strange turn of events.

Simpson had been on the phone almost constantly since he left the House but, when they dropped down on to the M4 proper from the elevated section, he at last replaced the handpiece.

'Sorry, Freddie, but it's best to do things when you get the prompting. Have you any appointments this evening?'

'Miracle of miracles, no. Normally I'm absolutely chocker block!'

'Good, then we can have supper with the Captain.'

'I'm surprised you invited this opposition rebel.'

'Freddie, I invited the man. Anyway you aired an important question and a real one. *Are* we too bloody selfish? And if we had the chance would we go for Justice or the big house?'

'Sobering question, but if we focus only on the downside we'll end up joining the law-of-the-jungle lot who think we're dressed-up savages.'

'So you're not wholly in the anti lobby?'

'I'm just bloody frustrated. Nothing ever happens. All we do is tinker, fiddle and talk – and, by God, we're good at that! Look at the schools. Teachers are leaving in despair and the experts still don't get it!'

'Ask the Captain about education.' Toby looked at Sharp directly. 'We need to tap the knowledge of these people.'

'I'm still sceptical,' Sharpe reacted, but he knew he was posturing.

They were both about the same age, yet Toby felt almost fatherly in his attitude.

'Freddie, you'll get over it!'

'It's not the flu I've got!'

They both laughed.

To Freddie Sharpe the whole situation was unreal. Not in his wildest moments could he have dreamt up such a story. Here he was about to meet the being/person that half the world was clamouring to see. And he hadn't even asked. He had to admit, though, that the uncritical attitude of the Minister had stopped him in his tracks; otherwise he would be still stoking his frustration.

'Minister, you were very reasonable at the despatch box. That really spiked my guns!'

'I don't know what came over me,' Toby joked. 'Freddie, we're both about the same age. It's Toby.'

'Thank you, Minister!'

They both burst out laughing.

*

At the entrance Freddie had to suffer the indignity of a body search and, of course, a comprehensive scan. The rules were strict. Only the PM, the Foreign Secretary and Toby were waved on. Even then they were careful, for look-alikes could not be discounted. So passwords were used and they changed frequently.

After leaving their briefcases in the hall, Toby suggested a walk. It would be refreshing after the drive from London and the earlier session in the House. Simpson also had another motive. He knew the Captain often took some exercise at this time, so he hoped for a spontaneous meeting where Freddie would be free of expectation and, in a sense, more open. This is exactly what happened, for in rounding a knot of bushes there was the Captain, examining some flowers.

'Ah, Toby, another beautiful day: Nature is so generous for every day is fresh and quite unique. You bring a friend, I see.'

'Captain, meet Frederick Sharpe MP, better known to his friends as Freddie.'

'Then, Sir, I'd better call you Freddie and join their number.'

'An honour, Captain, to have you on the list!'

There was a brief bubble of laughter as they shook hands.

'Let's walk, it's such a beautiful evening,' the Captain suggested easily.

Sharpe had gone beyond amazement. He was spellbound. His

world was practical, physical, with little time for notions of an esoteric kind. This being walking beside him was not ordinary, yet at the same time was very ordinary. His eyes, though, totally defied description. It was as if all wisdom dwelt there. Freddie had no neat, convenient answers.

'You both did well today. I watched it on the screen.'

'Toby was brilliant, but I, Sir, lost control.'

'Yes, but it worked well, so much so that some might think you'd planned it, which of course you didn't. It was genuine and it worked. Freddie, your honesty was most attractive.'

They walked on and Freddie felt it was on air. Toby, though, was fiddling with his handkerchief. His eyes were full again. The Captain's sensitive treatment of a somewhat vulnerable Freddie Sharpe had touched him.

All around the military presence was very obvious, yet they had deployed themselves discreetly. Was such a massive build-up necessary? It was probably the question every man was asking. Complacency clearly was the enemy, especially with such idyllic weather, for early June was certainly bursting out all over. Toby himself was sceptical. An attack seemed so totally improbable. Even so, intelligence was nervous. There were strange 'goings on' in central Asia, but that might mean anything. Nevertheless, both Vauxhall Cross and Langley were suspicious.

The stroll around the garden had been relaxing and the evening air had lent its renewing freshness. The Captain took his leave and Toby and his guest went to the kitchen to make some tea. The staff would not hear of it, so they retreated to the lounge to await a loaded tray.

'Well, what was your impression?' Simpson prompted.

'Toby, I was stunned and totally convinced. The Captain is a very special being.'

'What essential feeling do you get?'

'Goodness, Toby, sheer bloody goodness!'

Toby smiled. Freddie had his way of putting things.

'There's a lot of hardware around this place. Are they expecting World War Three?'

'They're concerned about kidnap and the Secret Service boys are edgy.'

'A suicide mission? It's possible. Land a few guys by sub; pick up the hardware at a prearranged dump, collected by their allies already resident. Then head for Winkfield.'

70

'Then what?'

'A tactic as old as time: create a diversion and then use your main force on the blind side as it were. I studied military history. Even so, it's a suicide mission. They'd never make the coast.'

Toby nodded pensively. The SIS had probably worked a similar game plan out but you could never tell. Better inform the PM about Freddie's analysis, but not by phone.

*

At supper the conversation flowed from subject to subject with seamless ease. Toby for the main kept silent for this was Freddie's evening. Eventually the conversation focused on education, with Freddie repeating what he had earlier said in the car.

'Teachers are retiring at fifty. They've had enough! The endless paperwork, the restrictions spawned by the paedophile obsession, the health and safety rules policed by eager officials, litigious parents, indeed violent parents, not to mention violence in the classroom, all pile in on them, and they dare not lift a finger. In fact, the more the violence grows, the more authority binds the teachers with restrictions. That's what my constituents constantly say. Often they are literally in despair. And, when I write to the department, I get a long academic spiel which is divorced completely from reality. My constituency isn't in a wealthy area, so few have recourse to private schooling. What can I do, Sir?'

'Freddie, I watched you in the House. You're fearless. Speak the truth, then truth itself will do your work.

'The principles of education are simple. They are embedded in your tradition: respect for the Supreme, respect for parents and respect for Nature, and for your neighbour's property. Then there are the prohibitions: do not lie, do not steal – your tradition holds it all. This is the foundation; the rest arises from it naturally.'

'I'll *need* to be fearless, Sir, for I'll be laughed to scorn!'

'Does it matter?'

'No!'

'What of punishment, Sir?' Freddie continued.

'Without punishment, authority is scorned, but punishment must never be from passion. It should be from love and in the child's best interest.'

'I'll need body armour on for that!' Sharpe reacted.

Simpson burst out laughing.

'After this, Freddie, the Chief Whip's a wimp!'

*

After taking Freddie home and reporting briefly to the PM, he set out again for Winkfield. The driver could have taken Freddie home, of course, but Simpson wanted to pass on Freddie's analysis of the kidnap threat. So it was almost midnight when Toby returned to Winkfield with his long-suffering driver, a well built ex-Army man with an uncomplaining sense of discipline.

'You're staying the night here, Bill, I hope?'

'Yes, Sir.'

'Good, then you'll join me in a nightcap.'

'Thank you, Sir.'

'You can't be seeing much of your family these days.'

'Yes, it's a bit busy, but I wouldn't change it, Sir!'

'Why, Bill?'

'Well, Sir, I'm not a religious man, but I feel blest when I'm in the Captain's company.'

'Yes, Bill, he's even getting through this hard-baked shell as well!'

Chapter Sixteen

Bill was an early riser, so as usual he was up and active. Indeed it was his favourite time to wash the car. Polishing he did throughout the day, during the waiting times. He was a big man, an Army man until a wound forced early but honourable retirement.

'Bill, you treat that car as if it were your daughter!'

'Good morning, Captain.' Bill hadn't seen the senior Visitor approach. He patted the car. 'Yes, she's a faithful old girl!'

The Captain chuckled.

'Bill, would you like to join me in an early cup of tea?'

'I would love to, Sir,' he responded, hanging his cloth on the side of the bucket.

'How're the children, Bill?' the Captain asked casually as they entered the house.

Bill was always amazed at the naturalness of the Captain. In fact, it was difficult to believe you weren't talking to your neighbour over the fence.

'They're fine, Sir, thanks for asking, but I am a bit worried at the time they spend listening to music and playing video games. I restrict the games but the music has got such a hold on them. It's this boom-boom stuff, and if I say a word they look at me as if I'm from another planet!' Suddenly, realising what he'd said, Bill stopped short and the Captain laughed heartily.

'Don't worry, Bill, I'll not report you to the PC lobby! Now, what you say is most unfortunate, for music has the power to calm or agitate the being. Young people are full of vigorous energy and they're drawn to violent rhythms. It's difficult to wean them off such habits once they've been established, but, if you yourself play better music in the home, these better strains may grow familiar. In fact the music itself will work. But any coercion in this area is mostly counter-productive.'

Nothing more was said on the subject and the Visitor moved the conversation to gardening. This was Bill's passion and the Captain listened intently to every word.

Later, when he told Toby Simpson about the early morning tea encounter, Bill was still full of amazement.

'It was as if he'd come deliberately from his distant star to talk to me. And now I feel so good about it, like a kind of sweetness. Minister, you must recommend some music, for I'm pretty hopeless in that area.'

*

With Air Force One touching down the following day, the media had grown obsessive. The press, although there were certainly exceptions, appeared to be competing with articles of foreboding. Having the Alien leader, the President and the PM present in one place provided the perfect terrorist moment, and as usual, they maintained, there was little preparation. So experts full of righteous rage were queuing up to savage the authorities. The rampant invective seemed confined to media ranks, and attacks on the Visitors, especially the Captain's so-called 'religious pomposity', were bitter and at times hysterical. What was going on? Something had stirred them up. What was it? Toby Simpson felt the answer close but couldn't put his finger on it.

Simpson left the papers to the side, while muttering that he'd frustrated and depressed himself enough. It was a beautiful morning and he had an hour or so before the Captain's first caller. What could he do? He could check his e-mails, but the thought had no appeal. What about the roof? He had never climbed the final steps before. Yes, why not? He could take his digital binoculars and have a look around, for the morning was ideal. Up he went, but halfway there he found it strange. What the devil was he doing here? There was no answer.

At the top the scene was clear, although the beginnings of a heat haze was filtering the light. What a view! Rolling park and farmland intermingled. There were footsteps to his right. He was not alone.

'Good morning, Brigadier.'

'Good morning, Minister. Enjoying the view?'

'Yes, good old English countryside: that farmstead is the only group of buildings we could say was close.'

'We have a presence there. The farmer doesn't mind for he knows we are his guardian angles.'

'You mean, the farmer could suddenly find a gun at his back, with a 'move over mate, your farm's our launching pad'?

'That's the better scenario!'

Simpson was scanning the scene with his binoculars.

'There's another farm over there.' He pointed. 'It's got a rather large shed and they're repairing it by the looks of things.'

'The Captain said the same the other day. His eyesight's very keen, you know.'

Toby was suddenly alerted.

'What did he say?'

'He just said "strange goings on" in a casual sort of way.'

'Brigadier, pardon me for meddling, but I'd check that farm place out and I'd make it a priority!'

'It's well out of range Minister.'

'Yes, for home-made mortars and the like, but not for PGMs!'

'They'd need a homing bug or some such bag of tricks. Who would plant that?'

'Maybe it's already planted. Remember we had rather hurried maintenance done!'

'It's most unlikely but we'll see to it. Anyway our boys and the CIA are arriving this morning, so they can check it out.'

'Sorry to be a pain!'

'You're not the pain, Minster, it's these damned terrorists. Last night my mind was plagued with scenarios. I hardly got a wink. And tomorrow – well, that frightens me. We've got "The Great Satan", the British PM and the Alien Infidel all in one place. They'll not be able to resist it!'

'Yes, it doesn't bare thinking about. Then there's the kidnap threat! And the media: they're so bloody negative!'

'The people aren't. A lot of folk are listening, Minister. I was in Windsor briefly yesterday and that was very obvious. I mean the people on the street.'

'Thanks, Brigadier, it's easy to be caught in a depressive litany. That, of course, helps no one.'

*

When Simpson returned to his office, Bill had already set out for Windsor to collect the New Zealand reporter who had featured positively at Westminster Hall. This was the Captain's first caller of the day, a quiet day in many ways before the coming storm.

He had forgotten the vanguard of the US security team, but their noisy arrival by helicopter soon changed that. Such an intrusion was often bitterly resented, but the initial edgy awkwardness was soon dispelled by the Brigadier's easy courtesy.

'Our American friends are here to ensure the safety of their President,' he told his own team, 'and we truly welcome all the help that we can get.'

The Americans responded with natural generosity and with little delay all got down to business. Unsurprisingly the US team was blessed with the latest gadgetry, so scanning the building for homing devices proceeded. Toby was relieved.

The Visitors failed to emerge during this noisy period. Simpson, however, had expected that, as it was their usual study period. Bill, he could see, had arrived at the gate and the New Zealand reporter was suffering the usual screening. Toby waited by the front entrance to receive him, and as he did the Brigadier came close.

'The SAS are moving in on the farm you pointed out. They don't, of course, advertise their presence but if there's trouble we'll probably hear. It's not that far away.' The Brigadier smiled thinly and moved on. The best of British, Toby thought.

At last the car was moving. Just then the unmistakable sound of rapid firing sounded in the distance. It lasted until the car had drawn up before the building. Then it suddenly stopped. The door opened and the big loose-limbed reporter stepped out.

'Welcome to Winkfield, Mr Sloane.'

'This *is* the treatment Mr Simpson!' The New Zealand accent was obvious, but all Toby could think of was the gunfire and his early morning exploration of the roof.

Chapter Seventeen

A news blackout was imposed on the incident at the farm, but Simpson was informed of all the details. A terrorist cell had been caught red-handed assembling sophisticated missiles. The resulting gun battle had been ferocious, with three of the terrorists killed outright. The other three fought recklessly until sharp-shooters immobilised them. At once the medics went to work. Intelligence wanted them alive. The owners, a retired farmer and his wife, escaped down the cellar, pulling the hatch after them and miraculously missing a hail of automatic fire. The terrorists fortunately hadn't followed but merely secured the hatch bolt. They were prudent for farmers did have shotguns. That was the sobering story at the farm. The story at the Manor House was also sobering. Two homing devices had been found, but they were of different origin. What did this mean? Did the terrorists merely pick up what they could? Or was there another cell? This was highly unlikely. Even so, the surrounding area would have to be covered. But who had planted the homing cells? That was the most disturbing question. Was the culprit a member of the staff or had he, or she, been amongst the local maintenance helpers? Then he remembered: there was one sure way to clear the household staff. He could use the Captain's ability to pick up darkness in the person. This was done as casually and unobtrusively as possible. Thankfully all, including the gardeners, responded guilelessly.

After consulting with the Brigadier, Toby decided to call the maintenance team in for 'emergency work' prior to the President's visit. It would sound feasible and the risk would be minimal, the Brigadier would see to that. The idea of a committed terrorist living in the area, and running lose, made both Toby and the Brigadier most uneasy. Everything that could be done had to be done. Perceived dangers simply could not be left until a more convenient time.

The maintenance team responded to the call much better than Toby had dreamed. In fact it turned out that they were all together in their van returning from a job when they received the call. For them the extra was a useful bonus.

The security routine at the gates was exhaustive and when the men were cleared they were asked to assemble near a ring of garden seats nearer to the Manor, where the Brigadier would address them. They might even see the Chief Visitor and the Minister Toby Simpson. All were duly impressed, and anyway they were being paid for it. 'Paid to swan around,' one said openly. They hadn't long to wait. For there they were, all three of them, walking briskly in their direction.

'We are most grateful for your prompt response, but alas we brought you here under false pretences.' The Brigadier smiled widely, looking at them all in turn. 'You see none of us expected that our Army engineers could do the job. So there you have it,' the Brigadier lied sweetly and the men laughed obligingly – that is, except for one who, even though he smiled, looked extremely tense. This was obvious to Toby and was readily confirmed by the Captain. They had found their man.

Later that evening, Simpson learned that the 'maintenance man' had been the leader and co-ordinator. The laptop in his Windsor garret flat had revealed it all. This was a find indeed, the ramifications of which could rumble on for months. The PGMs had been little more than damp squibs, for the electronics had been contaminated during their torturous journey; in any case they were primitive by modern standards. Three men had died for nothing but, of course, the promise of heaven was fervently believed. Toby had learned that the *Ksatriya* warrior class of Indian antiquity had held a similar belief, but death had to happen in a righteous war in which the rules of conduct were extremely strict. Indiscriminate terrorist killing clearly did not meet such requirements.

Before going to bed, Toby had an impulse to ring Drusilla and, instead of dismissing it as being too late, he obeyed.

'*Drusilla Cavendish-Browne.*'

'Drusilla, it's Toby Simpson obeying a sudden impulse to phone you.'

'*What a pleasant surprise.*'

'I have very little to tell you as my lips are permanently sealed.'

'*Oh, it's all right, Toby, if I want to know about you I simply watch the television!*'

Toby laughed; he liked the salty humour.

'*Lizzie and I went to the theatre last night and do you know who we bumped into?*'

'Tell me.'

'*Tom Wynter and his lady and Richard, that rather nice brother of Tom.*'

'Methinks I have a rival!'

'*Methinks your sister has a beau. They got on like a house on fire.*'

'Well, well. Had they met before?'

'*Don't think so. It was rather like "across a crowded room" and all that business!*'

'Good for Lizzie. I like Richard, but of course I know Tom better; we went to school together. Anyway we're all meeting up shortly for the panel.'

'*Tom called it his Waterloo!*'

'I hope he's Wellington!'

'*He feels like Napoleon at the moment, he told me, but was aiming for the Iron Duke on the night!*'

'Well, we'll be there with the cavalry! Sorry, Drusilla someone's knocking. It's probably about tomorrow. I'd better sign off... Coming!' he called out as a head appeared at the door.

'*I'd better let you go, thanks for calling and call again.*'

'Stop me if you can! Bye, Drusilla.'

'*Bye.*'

The door opened to reveal one of the Brigadier's ADCs.

'The Americans are worried about these media rumours on the late news.'

'Right, let's see them,' Toby responded.

'The Americans were grouped around the TV.'

'What's been happening?' he asked.

'The late night news is full of rumours. And your fellas simply say "No comment"! This could upset the folks back home.'

'It's all right, gentlemen. We bagged a big fish, but it's under wraps. Even I'm under wraps! We don't want to give the bad boys any publicity, hence no comment, OK?'

'Hey, some of you guys give Toby a glass. I told you, the Brits know what they're doin'. They're good at this. And hey, it's their patch!'

'But Ed...'

'Wrap it up guys! OK?'

Toby felt he needed to clear the air.

'It's like this, gentlemen: if we told the press the happenings of the day AQ would stand to gain too much publicity, for even if it's bad publicity, it's still publicity. So we button up occasionally. Tomorrow the stage is set for your President and our honoured guest, the Captain. It's their day for publicity! The media, of course, will scratch around. That's the freedom of the press. Sometimes I have other words for it! But I didn't say it!'

'We got it, Toby. Hey, fill that glass.'

'That's it, gentlemen. I have to meet your President tomorrow and I need to be reasonably sane.'

'It's OK, Toby, he's only a Democrat!'

They all laughed.

Chapter Eighteen

Despite elaborate preparations at Heathrow, Air Force One diverted to Brize Norton. The RAF base was infinitely quieter, with only a limited media presence. Of course, security chiefs were always trying ways to thwart potential terrorists, but this time there'd been a warning from a trusted source.

Bob Shaw was waiting on the apron to greet his friend Sam Gilmore. Initially it would be Mr President and Mr Prime Minister, but once settled in the limo it would be Bob and Sam.

The whine of the engines had slowly died and Air Force One was now at rest like some sleek bird, passive yet completely certain of its supper. Slowly and deliberately security staff moved closer to take up their positions. Only a fool or a fanatic would dare to be inquisitive! The door opened and there was his friend, as upright and well groomed as ever, holding his wife's hand firmly as they descended to the apron.

'Welcome, Mr President, and to your lovely lady.'

'Thank you, Prime Minister; it's good to be in Oxfordshire, the home to many of my youthful pranks!'

They stood as 'The Star Spangled Banner' was intoned, but that was the limit of formality. It was not an official state visit and both men had agreed to keep the detail simple.

'Mary's waiting in the car,' Shaw explained. 'She's sorry not to see you arriving but she finds standing difficult. It can excite her back problem.'

'Bob, no offence is even dreamed of. Now, what do you propose?'

'That we go in your limo, Sam, for that will keep your security boys happy.'

'That'll be the day. They're all card-carrying pessimists! OK let's saddle up. I hope you've planned a scenic route!'

Shaw's eye caught sight of the huge US transporter, it's wings drooping as if weary.

'Your limo arrived some hours ago and apparently a route was agreed. They're avoiding the Oxford ring road and the A34 and have chosen a surprising route via Cirencester and Swindon to the M4.'

'I know it; they're going via Bibury. Jeez, this is a bonus. The roads are a bit narrow, but hey, we could have a coffee!'

'I feel a nightmare coming on!'

'Bob, I went to Oxford. Some of my best years were spent round here. I'm the US President for God's sake. Can't I have a goddam coffee?'

*

The limo slipped through the countryside with effortless ease. Mary Shaw and Jenny Gilmore who had met frequently were busy in conversation, leaving the men to deliberate about the day ahead. Though he had expected it, Shaw was pleased with Gilmore's attitude, for it was clear that the President was not burdened with pomposity or petty pre-conceived ideas.

The coffee stop was on, but Shaw was not overly concerned; no 'bad boys' could have guessed their route. A few of the Americans had gone ahead to make arrangements, including the President's Press Officer, for as far as he was concerned this was heaven-sent PR. Having dropped the party near the coffee lounge, the drivers tucked the limos off the street just across the bridge. The locals had been most obliging. For Gilmore the break was all too short, yet he savoured every moment like a lover. Shaw was amused but rather touched and felt his sense confirmed that Gilmore would appreciate the Captain.

Once on the dual carriageway, the traffic police controlled the traffic and when they reached the M4 the road was empty; all traffic had been gradually brought to a halt. Shaw had witnessed the technique many times. The three police cars used for the slowing process now straddled the road, their blue lights flashing as the Presidential cavalcade swept on to the carriageway. Shaw could just see the flashing lights in the mirror. They were moving and slowly they would build up speed again, but stay at the regulation distance.

'Have you any advice, Bob? I mean about the Captain, as you call him,' Gilmore asked after being pensive for some time.

'Ask questions, the fundamental ones. This being, person, call him what you like, has great wisdom – and, Sam, he lives it!'

'The fellas tell me that you had a little spot of trouble,' the President continued.

'Yes, we were very lucky, and what's more we bagged the ringleader. His hard disk is a gold mine! It's all under wraps, but no doubt Langley will be kept informed.'

'What goes with these guys?' Sam Gilmore shook his head.

'Love has been usurped by hate. It's ugly!'

'It sure is!'

'If only we could hear the moderate voice more often.'

'Bob, you need brave men for that. The loudmouth gang are out for power. They have it easy: the young are drawn to their passionate rants like bees to honey.'

'You describe it all too well.'

'Here we are, allegedly two of the most powerful leaders in the world, but what can we do? No matter what the measure, opposition seems to spring from nowhere like a pop-up book!'

'Yet, despite it all, it's quite amazing how we muddle through!'

'Well, Bob, I think we've got enough to ask the Captain!'

The President's limo still cruised on with silent ease while, on the other carriageway, the endless stream of vehicles were speeding by like arrows. Shaw could see the police cars' blue lights still flashing, just as they had been since the cavalcade reached the motorway. A sharp drop on speeding tickets today, he thought with amusement. The ladies were still talking but, apart from the occasional comment, the two leaders were content to rest.

Shaw had questioned the wisdom of diverting to Brize Norton, for it wasted so much time, but security had feared an incident and that was that. Anyway, it had given the President time to settle in – and he'd had his coffee! Again, the conversation had been useful.

They had just past Maidenhead; soon it would be Slough and the Windsor exit. Lunch would be waiting. Shaw felt hungry.

Chapter Nineteen

All the paraphernalia needed for television was in place. It was to be a live broadcast, with the cameras of four TV networks focused on the dais. As the main meeting was planned for later in the afternoon, it was scheduled as a brief event. Nevertheless it was important, being the first introduction of the Alien Chief to the President of the United States. The viewing figures could be astronomic.

Toby Simpson was almost eerily calm. Anticipating events seemed so utterly childish; things would happen when they happened. His even-mindedness amazed him as much as anyone else. There could only be one explanation: the daily company of the Captain.

Toby and the Brigadier stood together, along with the US security chief. First to show itself was the leading police car, then two stretch limos, followed by a smaller limo, no doubt full of security men. The President had arrived. Toby stepped forward.

'Welcome, Mr President.'

'Thank you, Mr Simpson – your person is well known to me, for every day I see you on the screen.'

'Well, Sir, I'd better tell my agent to increase my fee!'

Gilmore's laugh was full.

'Sir, the cameras are set up for the initial greetings, but before that would you like to freshen up, as they say.'

'Excellent idea, we'll return duly refreshed in ten minutes.' Again he laughed.

Bob Shaw nodded as he passed. It was a father's nod, pleased with the progress of a son.

'Jeez, Toby, how do you do it? The President can be very formal,' Ed Banks, the American security chief, rasped.

'Ed, it was that whiskey you handed out last night! Listen, I'd better go and get the Captain.'

Still Toby felt relaxed and calm. There was no eager rush to find the Captain. He simply walked.

*

84

It was the Captain's detached ease that held Simpson's attention. The whole unfolding drama of the reception ceremony was played perfectly. Both the President and the Prime Minister were on their home territory, as it were, but the Captain was from another planet! Indeed, moment by moment, the Captain's actions were his teacher.

The reception ceremony was brief but it satisfied the White House Press Office. All knew that the one-to-one in the afternoon would carry the real substance. A buffet lunch was next, when the President mingled with the hand-picked guests – for with two serious attempts and an incident frustrated at Heathrow security was near to paranoiac. The foreign secretary Sir James Huntington was present, as was the American Ambassador, together with the Canadian High Commissioner and the leader of the opposition. Indeed the guests were very few, which made Freddie Sharpe's presence all the more unusual. Sensing that Freddie felt like a fish out of water, and also that his party leader seemed to be avoiding him, Toby Simpson purposely engaged him in conversation.

'What the hell am I doing here, Toby?' Freddie burst out.

'The Captain – "Is Freddie coming?" he asked. So here you are.'

'The Captain?!'

'Yes, the Captain.'

'That day changed me, Toby. You know, the day you brought me here.'

'In what way?'

'It's difficult to explain. It's like waking up after you've been dreaming, or like emerging from a fog!'

'Shakespeare's "pale cast of thought" – you know the line?'

'Toby, I've always thought that Shakespeare was for toffs!'

Simpson laughed, and at the same time he could see Hugh Herbert, the opposition leader, heading towards them.

'Freddie, your boss is coming over.'

'I'm in his bad books at the moment!'

Herbert was a big man, overweight, yet fairly nimble on his feet.

'What are you two conspiring about?' he boomed.

'We couldn't possibly tell you, Sir; if we did, we wouldn't be conspirators!' Toby quickly countered.

Herbert rumbled, but he had just caught the eye of the

Archbishop of Canterbury. 'Sorry, gentlemen, Lambeth Palace is smiling so I must obey! And Freddie...', he added, patting Sharpe's arm, 'leave this education thing alone, it's a no-no!'

Simpson said nothing. The relationship between Freddie and his party leader was none of his business. Freddie, though, had no such inhibitions.

'They don't want to know. I suggested exploratory talks on a cross-party consensus, but they don't want to know!'

'Are you surprised?

'Part of me is not, but the other part, the new Sharpe as it were, thought they would see what I *now* see as blindingly obvious. I tried to be as "softly, softly" as possible – in other words, not the usual Freddie Sharpe – but the education boys thought the Captain's ideas were medieval. In fact they listened with an amused incredulity. I almost blew up, but I didn't. Instead I picked my papers up, thanked them for listening and left.'

'Definitely a reformed Sharpe ... Hey,' he added in a confidential whisper, 'the President's on his way.'

'Ah, the men of the future!' Gilmore's drawl was friendly.

'That begs a question, Mr President: do we deserve your sympathy or applause?' Toby Simpson asked easily.

'My applause as you rise to meet the challenge; my sympathy at the roughness of the road, for the modern highwaymen have more than pistols! Now, Sir, may I call you Toby?'

'Of course, Mr President, and may I introduce Freddie Sharpe MP?'

'Freddie, good to know you.'

'You may change your mind, Sir, when you know the detail!'

The President chuckled.

'Ah, a man of wit and presence!'

'Mr President, you've escaped my tutelage again!' The Prime Minister was suddenly upon them.

'Not another night in Paddington Green!'

The Prime Minister's sudden gust of laughter caught the gathering's attention but the buzz of conversation soon arose again.

'Freddie here wants to rescue education from the party policy arena. How did you put it, Freddie? "A football kicked about by rival academics who talk as though they'd never seen the inside of a classroom!" A bit colourful, Freddie, but you certainly made your mark!'

'A very small mark, Sir: the sacred cows of *them* and *us* are strong.'

'A point well made, Freddie. Gentlemen, the Captain and his Deputy have just walked through the door... So, Mr President, I feel we should make ourselves available.'

'Well, what my mentor tells me I must do!' the President chuckled. 'Keep batting, Freddie. That's the term we used to use in my Oxford student days. And, Freddie, if you're ever stateside, look me up. You probably know my address!' The President grinned widely. 'And, Toby, you're included in the package. That goes without saying!'

'Thank you, Mr President.' The voices were almost in unison.

'Isn't it rich?' Freddie burst out. 'The PM is more supportive than my own party boss!'

'That's not unusual! Party leaders need to keep their party united, and in opposition that's not easy. Freddie, you're causing the poor man a lot of hassle!'

They both stood silent for some time, watching the scene. Lunch they knew was imminent.

'Are you still concerned about a kidnap attempt?' Freddie asked.

'We are. We followed up your idea of an equipment dump but nothing has been found. They're still searching but security is very stretched, especially with the President in our midst. Ah, lunch at last!'

Chapter Twenty

Apparent chaos preceded the televised *tête-à-tête* between the Captain and the President, but from previous experience Toby Simpson knew that such supposed confusion was misleading for the professionals were indeed professional. So when the Captain and the President took their seats all was in place and ready.

The cameras panned in close.

'Sir,' the President began, 'I am awed by the technical achievements of your people, but now that I have met you I know a greater wonder: your tranquillity and peace. How, Sir, can we learn from your wisdom?'

'Mr President, you have it all, for your libraries hold the wisdom of the ages: the great universal singularity, expounded by the master teachers, that there is one and only one. Krishna, Plato and Christ all taught the same; the same the Sufi masters knew.'

'Some seem to claim exclusive ownership of the truth. Such passions sweep the Earth with war. What is your answer, Sir?'

'Tradition is the radiance of the Supreme and to claim a single ray as being exclusive is unreasonable.'

The President bowed his head. What could he say? For exclusivity in some form was the claim of most religions. Indeed to say anything was a sure way to offend someone! He changed the subject.

'Sir, when you met the international press at Westminster Hall, you made the arresting statement that sometimes in your country the post of Chief Elder was allowed to lapse because no one had reached a sufficient level of humility. I have played the recording many times and every time your statement gives me the tantalising feeling of being close to something, some fresh understanding. Can you say more on this, Sir?'

'Your great teacher Socrates was considered wise. Indeed the Delphic Oracle stated that there was no one wiser than Socrates. Socrates was puzzled, for he knew he wasn't wise – but then, the Oracle never lied. So what was, or rather is, the solution?'

'I've heard the answer, Captain. Socrates was the wisest of men because he knew that only God is wise. Only now have I got some sense of what that really means, and also what is meant by true humility. Thank you, Sir.'

It was time, the President felt, to introduce a lighter note. Being a consummate politician, he knew the moment.

'Captain, I spent some very happy years at Oxford where they struggled hard to educate me, so I know and love this country. You have chosen well, but we would also do you proud. I do believe the White House has a few spare rooms!'

'The East Room in the morning would be nice.' The Captain's smile was manifestly mischievous.

The President laughed, amazed at the Alien leader's grasp of detail.

'Mr President, you're wondering how I know such things?'

'I guess I am.'

'The answer, Sir, a library book!'

Gilmore laughed again.

'There you got it. That's how molehills shoot up into mountains.'

'Sir, the Americans are a generous people and you, their President, have honoured us by flying here at no little inconvenience. But regretfully we cannot accept your kind offer. If we were to visit you, we would clearly be obliged to visit others, and where might we hope to make an end? There are, of course, the security hazards imposed by endless travel. I trust you understand that no offence is meant.'

'No offence is taken, Captain, none at all. But may I ask you a further question?'

The Chief Visitor nodded.

'My good friend the British Prime Minister questioned you on economic matters and your answer excited much debate in our media. The majority dismissed the community-created rent-collection theory as hopelessly impractical. Some progressive elements didn't seem to understand it, but there was a grouping that was most enthusiastic, one might say embarrassingly so. They were followers of our own American economist Henry George. Indeed, it seems to be an issue that excites the strongest of emotions. Are there any further comments you might like to make?'

'Our system of location rent collection has been applied for many generations. Simple competition establishes the rate, but there are laws protecting continuity of tenure. Indeed callous evictions are frowned upon. This is the sole revenue of the state except for donations in times of difficulty or for special projects. These are given willingly. Only in a crisis is there a compulsory collection. We do not tax the labour of the citizen or any entrepreneurial grouping, so our citizens enjoy the full reward of their labour. This, and easy access to land on payment of location rent, releases the natural energies of the citizen. So there are many entrepreneurs and, because of that, great demand for labour, which of course keeps earnings at a maximum.

'Both education and health care are paid for by the citizens who, due to this, can exercise their preferences. Treatment delays, for instance, would not be tolerated. This is a very brief summary of our system. It works for us; you, of course, may evolve something quite different, but the laws will be the same, for in all cases location value belongs to the community. Indeed, without the community there would be no value. To put it very simply: that which is created by the community belongs to the community and that which is created by the individual is proper to the individual. This we perceive to be the natural law.' The Chief Visitor smiled knowingly. 'Mr President, I hope I haven't lulled all our viewers to sleep.'

'That's my speciality, Sir!'

The President briefly took a sip of water.

'Captain, there are many questions. For example: are your cities similar to ours? Are your houses similar? What is the nature of your agriculture? We'd all be most interested in some brief outline. And, of course, we are now belatedly aware of environmental problems. Do you have such concerns?' Such questions the President knew would lighten the rather concentrated diet.

The Captain replied in detail on the nature of the average household and the more locally integrated farm marketing arrangements.

'Our cities are similar to here but not so densely packed,' he continued. 'Our sliding-scale rent system encourages a much more even spread throughout the country.' The Visitor followed on with an outline of living habits, which in the main were strangely similar to those on Earth. However there was one

90

recurring feature: the pace of life in every case appeared to be much slower.'

'Sir, you appear to have a much less pressured life than us,' the President interjected.

'We are a placid people, but we admire your fire and enthusiasm. We don't have your fierce competitive environment and, except for things like bottles, mass-production lines are rare. In fact, our manufacturers and artisans compete on quality. Of course, the price needs to be reasonable, but it's not the vital factor.'

'So you're not a throw-away society?'

'"Throw-away"? Yes, I see. You almost got me, Sir! Mr Simpson keeps a count, you know!'

They both chuckled.

'What you've just said throws much light on the environmental issue. Have you any other words to say on this?'

'Window dressing, as it's aptly called, is of little use. We need to nurture and apply a reverence for Nature. This is the keystone of it all.'

The President was more than satisfied. Such words from this amazing being's lips were worth a thousand lectures.

The producer was signalling. It was time for final words.

✳

The President sat back in his chair, feeling completely at ease.

'Well, Captain, I'm told I have two hours before I need to leave for Windsor. There I need to be on time for I'm dining with Her Majesty. Two hours, Captain, it's unprecedented – usually every minute is a prisoner! So, if it fits with your arrangements, we could have a further chat, and as we're both in England we can have a cup of tea!'

'May I suggest a walk, the gardens are quite lovely; and after that tea would be most welcome.'

'Great! My security boys may be lurking but I guess you'll not mind that!'

Chapter Twenty-One

The press were vicious. Toby Simpson had never known it so bad. It was as if they'd totally lost control or, even worse, had been possessed. 'Tree-hugging Alien describes primitive society while sycophantic President grovels'. Then there was the usual card-carrying anti-American rubbish. Were these the people who informed us in their daily columns? Their blatant arrogance was insufferable.

Toby was about to vent his ire on the Downing Street press office when the phone rang.

'Toby, turn to Breakfast Time.' At once the phone went dead.

Toby pressed the remote and there was the PM, looking anything but pleased, being addressed by the familiar self-satisfied icon.

'Prime Minster, this morning's press are almost unanimous in condemning yesterday's rather pathetic performance at Winkfield?'

'Are "pathetic performance" your words?' Shaw barked.

'Well, yes,' the media man said hesitantly.

'Did you listen to the interview?' The PM was clearly angry.

'Yes.' Again the note was hesitant.

'The whole interview?'

The interviewer seemed confused.

'Be careful, Sir.'

'I saw the relevant excerpts.'

'Who decided they were relevant?'

'The team.'

'I see, it's all a little vague. Well, perhaps I've been a little harsh, but I'll make a deal. I'll introduce you to the Captain. Then you can make your own mind up first-hand. Do you agree?'

'It's a very generous offer, Prime Minister. Yes.'

The Prime Minister felt weary. Losing his cool, to use the current jargon, had been very foolish. He had gone to the studio to try and counter the madness, but instead he'd simply made things worse. Striding out of the studio he headed for the waiting Jaguar and gratefully slumped into the back seat. Almost immediately the phone rang.

'Shaw.'

'Prime Minister, that was brilliant!'

'What do you mean, Toby? I lost my temper!'

'You've woken people up. They might even read the script!'

'I'd better ring the President. When's he leaving?'

'Midday.'

'Dammit! I'll go to Brize Norton. It'll show solidarity, and maybe I'll get a sleep in the back of the Jaguar!'

'You'll be lucky!'

The Prime Minister made two phone calls and all was set in motion. He sank back into the seat, content to let the professionals do their job. The car had not moved from its VIP slot but Shaw was unconcerned, for he guessed that they were waiting for the police car escort.

When he was a boy he had seen Harold Macmillan walking across the pedestrian crossing at Victoria on his way to the station without a minder in sight. We had come a long way from those simple days.

The phone rang just as he saw the reflection of a blue light flashing on the plate class of the nearby building.

'Bob, that was great!' It was the President.

'Sam, I lost my temper.'

'Nope, you were forceful but controlled!'

'Sam, you've got the job, my PR man!'

There was a chuckle down the line.

'I'm seeing you off at Brize Norton. It'll show a united front.'

'Thanks, Bob. Well, I'll see you there. Say, what's got into the press. They've all shot into orbit.'

'It's a good question. Have your theory ready when I see you!'

There was another chuckle and then the phone went dead.

The car was already on the move and approaching Hanger Lane. Shaw had plenty of time. Maybe he could have a coffee! His son had told him of a garden centre that served home-made cakes. Mary wouldn't approve, of course. He smiled to himself. Then he thought of the police car and the outriders. It wasn't on. Well, why not for heaven's sake? As his friend the President would say, 'We can all have a goddam coffee!' It would give the press something to gossip about. And, in any case, he liked meeting people in this way. After all, he was an MP, a representative of the people.

*

They were already loading the President's limo into the transporter when the Prime Minister arrived. Almost at once he spotted the President on the apron, busy chatting to the technicians and security men. Close by the TV people were setting up for the low-key send-off. As for other visitors, there were none. Even the American Ambassador was absent in France. The lack of fuss was partly due to the President but mostly at the wish of security. Numerous warnings had made them very edgy. This was evidenced by the endless burr of helicopters.

'Let's escape into the bird. We've fifteen minutes before the game starts. Those choppers make it impossible!'

Inside Air Force One the sudden silence was tangible.

'Well, Mr President, what's your theory? Why is the press so adolescent?'

'Jeez, Bob, gimme time!'

Shaw grinned and Gilmore peered through a nearby window in a sightless sort of way.

'You know, Bob, the Captain is a truly good person. He radiates goodness and at one time yesterday I felt like weeping. Imagine, a hard bitten guy like me.'

'That's what Toby Simpson tells me! He sees the Captain daily and one day, he says, he'll not be able to control it!'

'Well, Bob, here's my theory: when the light increases, the creatures in the dark become exposed and *that* they do not like.'

'My God, Sam, I think you've hit the button!' Shaw exhaled noisily. 'Security is at screaming pitch already but it's as clear as day, we can't let up.'

'When are they leaving?'

'I've never asked them, Sam. My brass neck isn't brass enough, but maybe I should. Not yet though!'

Sam Gilmore laughed and Bob Shaw quickly joined him.

'Well, Bob, let's do this official thing.'

94

Chapter Twenty-Two

Eating humble pie had been worth it, Jim Billing thought with smug satisfaction. No other TV presenter had been allowed near Winkfield, but he was on his way. OK, the PM had cut him up a bit, but such things happened. Anyway, the bottom line was an interview with the Alien. That was a coup.

Billing's familiar sharp-featured face made no difference to the rigorous security check; no detail was omitted. For heaven's sake, everybody knew who he was! What was the big deal? He was annoyed and it showed in his body language, but he had sufficient sense to keep his mouth shut. What made it worse was the special way they treated the idiot Freddie Sharpe. He was simply waved through. Again Billing made no comment. Comments would come later on prime time. That would be fun!

Next Billing met the new boy, Simpson – born with a silver spoon and typical of that privileged bunch. He was offered tea and accepted while wondering when the Vicar and the cucumber sandwiches would arrive.

'Sorry, Jim,' Simpson apologised, 'we're running a bit behind. Freddie's with the Captain and that can take a little time.' Simpson smiled knowingly and Billing managed to reciprocate.

Toby was concerned. Had the PM been in error in allowing the TV icon access, for his arrogance was palpable? Well, the Prime Minister had promised on Breakfast TV and that was that. No doubt the Captain would handle things, but Toby was uneasy. He didn't trust the TV celebrity and, unusually, he decided to sit in on the interview.

Eventually Freddie emerged, smiling broadly, and after apologising for any delay he walked out into the garden.

'I'll see you later, Toby,' he called out airily from the door.

Toby went into the Captain's room and returned almost immediately to where Billing was waiting, confident and full of questions. Where's your spacecraft? Why are you afraid to show it? Here you meet world leaders and those approved by government: why don't you meet the ordinary working people?

'Jim, you're on!'

Billing strode in purposively, followed quietly by Toby who introduced the TV presenter and retired to the side of the room.

'You ran into a little trouble this morning, Mr Billing, but then without that I probably would not have had the pleasure of meeting you.'

Uncharacteristically, Billing could not think of a riposte.

'Now, Sir, can I ask you a question?' The Captain continued quietly.

Billing nodded, his mind captured by the Alien's eyes: they were so passive, so free of calculation.

'Why are the media so excessive in their comments?'

Billing had not expected this. He was the one who asked the questions!

'They are disturbed, Sir,' Billing said plainly. God, what was he saying?

'I think you have more to say, Mr Billing.'

'Well, Sir, they see your message as a threat.'

'To what, Mr Billing?'

'To their way of life and thinking.' Billing's assertive confidence seemed to have deserted him. Like a troubled climber he could find no hand or footholds and the questions that he had been nurturing would not formulate. The Alien's pool-like eyes were like a mirror in which Billing seemed to see his own persona as a stranger. The pretension was so obvious.

The Captain's smile still beamed on the broadcaster.

'What threat do *you* perceive, Sir?'

Billing knew he could not posture, not with those eyes gazing at him.

'I saw Victorian authority and unwanted discipline.' Billing paused, hesitant like a diver on the high board just before he plunges. 'Now I see no threat.' My God, his old self thought: how easily you betray your own. Suddenly his past rose up in protest. 'This isn't easy, Sir!'

The eyes of the Alien were still smiling.

'Yes, Mr Billing, but once you jump the hurdle it's behind you.'

Billing's sudden agitation waned and then he knew the peace he'd known only as a child. Something deep within had turned its face to reason.

'Mr Billing...'

'Please call me Jim, Sir!'

Toby Simpson gulped and almost lost control.

'Well, Jim, all three of us, I feel, should have a walk. The gardens here are beautiful. I never tire of them.'

Toby could hardly believe it, for it had happen so quickly, just like the throwing of a switch. There were no long reflections or debates. Yet he was certain that Jim Billing had changed. It was in a sense his Damascene Road.

*

Billing liked gardens and was an expert when it came to plants imported in the heady days of colonial dominance. The Captain listened intently, absorbing the Latin tags like an everyday language and, when the Captain quoted the Latin plant names back to him, Billing was amazed. If he had needed further proof, then this was it. The Captain, as Toby Simpson called him, was remarkable. In fact, a more impressive being he had never met.

When the walk was over it was time to leave, for he had a broadcast in the evening.

'When are you coming to see us again, Jim?' the Captain asked.

'I would be honoured, Sir, but when should...?'

'Same time, in two days' time: so far that day's fairly free. Does that suit, Jim?'

'I'll make it suit!'

Toby Simpson saw Billing off at the entrance and when he returned the Captain was waiting at the front of the building.

'Toby, you have never invited you sister and her lovely friend to visit me?'

'Well, Sir, I felt I couldn't exploit my position to serve personal wishes.'

'I would like to see them, Toby.' The Captain's mischievous look was not disguised. Then he went inside.

Toby was about to follow when he saw the Brigadier rushing towards him.

'Minister, there's been a worrying development on the Dorset coast. Apparently an insomniac retired naval veteran spotted a submarine offshore unloading half a dozen men. A lighthouse light exposed them in a pulse-like way. So our insomniac alerted an MOD friend of his. The bad news is, it wasn't our submarine. The good news is, the SAS are on to it.'

'The press?'

'They don't know – yet! The locals have been complaining about helicopter noise but that's all.'

'My God, this is serious ... and the implications!'

'I know, state-sponsored stuff ... not nice!'

'Thank God for the insomniac!'

Chapter Twenty-Three

They found the dingy secreted in a rock cave by the shore. Seaweed had been used as camouflage and it was judged that the intruders expected to return. The problem was that they had disappeared. What was more, there were no clues whatever regarding their intention.

To Toby's way of thinking drugs were out. Submarines were not for hire. Bribery could of course corrupt a commander, but what about the crew? No, the whole scenario was too improbable. So who in God's name were they? Was this the mad kidnap plot or was it terrorism and, if that were the case, was it state-sponsored? Impossible questions, all of which seemed to hatch the most improbable answers.

*

The Premier revealed the situation to a full meeting of the Cabinet. Only Toby Simpson and the Northern Ireland Secretary were absent. He quickly looked round the table. How many could he really trust? The Foreign Secretary, the Home Secretary and the Defence Secretary: they were solid. The others would blow with the wind. And the Chancellor? Well, he was too overindulged to blow anywhere, but the Premier didn't trust him, not one little bit, and he had his cronies willing to oblige his every whim. The 'useful idiots' Shaw thought, recalling Lenin's cynicism.

The Cabinet was as leaky as a sieve. He was loath reveal anything to do with security but he had to tell them something.

'They landed someway near to George's bathing hut,' the PM quipped. The Chancellor grinned but Shaw could see he didn't like it. Everyone knew George Gribbones had a cottage near Lyme Regis which was rather well appointed as the press were keen in listing the extravagances. 'Golden George buys golden taps' was now a quoted headline.

'Why can't we send these Aliens packing?' The Environment Secretary said with some impatience. 'There's been nothing but trouble since they came!'

'Hear, hear!' two other members echoed, while at least three others nodded. This was not lost on the Prime Minister.

The Chancellor sat impassively, pretending to be unimpressed.

Shaw scanned those seated round the Cabinet table, his thoughts anything but conciliatory. George's little army had foolishly revealed themselves.

'Had you considered that they might not scamper to their Alien home, but simply choose another country here on Earth? You may be able to suggest one!' The PM's irony was not disguised and no one was foolish enough to reply. 'How many of you have met the Captain?' He knew the answer, of course: the Foreign Secretary, the Home Secretary, the Defence Secretary and the leader of the House. They immediately raised their hands.

'Who else would like to go?' Shaw pressed. 'Seeing these remarkable beings face to face is an experience!'

Two more, including the Trade and Industry Secretary, raised their hands.

'Why not bring them here?' the Chancellor grumbled after some delay. 'It would save a lot of hassle!'

Four heads nodded vigorously and Shaw knew he had his confirmation. The fox cubs had shown themselves!

'Security, George. As I've told you, things are pretty tight at present!'

The Chancellor was clearly unconvinced.

'Prime Minister, all of us are potential targets! Why are we allowed to walk the streets and take foolhardy risks? What makes these Aliens so special and so ultra-vulnerable that they need such paranoid security? I wish somebody could tell me that!'

'Good question, George, and one that's difficult to answer other than to say that terrorists love publicity and something new and uniquely exclusive would be a perfect target. Eliminating heathens like the Prime Minister and the Chancellor, who could quickly be replaced, is one thing, but assassinating the Alien Captain would be unique.'

'He's got a Deputy!'

'Yes, George,' the PM sighed. 'Golden Taps' as the press had nicknamed him, was getting tedious. 'We've a duty to protect our visitors. End of story!'

The next item on the agenda was the rising spectre of inflation and the Prime Minister listened patiently as the Chancellor trotted out the fashionable answers as if he had invented them. God, how had he been fooled into thinking that this balding hulk was an authority? But there it was and he was saddled with him. The trouble was Gribbones had a following and, knowing the latest security briefing, Shaw knew he dared not risk a party squabble. A posse of National and Commonwealth leaders were due, which was a further reason to keep the ship on even keel.

Gribbones droned on. For Shaw the tedium was unbearable.

'Chancellor, we all bow before your undoubted authority, but can you tell me in simple words what the interest rise and tax increases will achieve?'

'It will slow down the economy which at present is in danger of overheating.'

'Can I test your patience? Why will it slow it down?

'Because borrowing will become more expensive.'

'I'm sorry, Chancellor, but what does that mean?'

'Hopefully it means that the economy will begin to slow down and inflationary pressures will ease.'

'And what effect will the slow-down have?'

'It will stabilise the economy. But, Prime Minister, you know all this!'

'George, I've heard it, but it doesn't mean I know it.' Shaw smiled. 'Can I test your patience further? What effect will this have on the ground?'

'Prices will stay firm, which will keep the housewife happy.' Gribbones grinned.

'You've been more than patient, Chancellor, but surely there must be some other telling effects?'

'Labour costs should flatten out, one hopes. Stiffer competition for jobs would see to that.'

'Is that a way of saying unemployment would rise?'

'Yes, there'd be a rise, marginal one hopes. But, PM, you've heard all this many times. What are you trying to say?'

'Fair point, George. Now this is a question I have often asked and one that excited the most convoluted answers. Is unemployment necessary for a healthy economy?'

'Prime Minister, that's an unfair question. No one desires unemployment, but some restraints need to be imposed. It is a complicated issue. Indeed, in the early 2000s we had full employment and minimal inflation.'

'Yes Chancellor,' Tom Gibb the Home Secretary interjected, 'but we had a massive cheap labour intake, and skilled labour too, from Eastern Europe. What plumber isn't Polish?'

Gribbones hesitated, leaving the Prime Minister to respond.

'Most interesting, Tom: so you're saying that full employment and low inflation were possible because cheap labour had the same effect as unemployment. Even I can understand that!'

Gribbones' smile was thin. He didn't like Gibb's intervention, not at all.

*

The thought of half a dozen dedicated terrorists hiding some-where undetected distracted the PM considerably. There had been many secret warnings on his watch but this somehow was the most disturbing. The involvement of a submarine spelled state sponsorship or, even worse, a rogue element in some military regime, perhaps with the connivance of some ruling faction. How did the minds of these guys work? Something motivated them – something they'd been taught, something that they'd taken to heart when young. All at once a line from an American musical repeated – it was completely spontaneous: 'You've got to be taught, carefully taught, to hate all the people your relatives hate.' Maybe those weren't the exact words but they were near enough. Was it the teachers who were to blame? If so, who had taught the teachers? Somehow, somewhere, someone had to wake up and remember his or her humanity, otherwise there was no hope. Shaw was in his office pacing up and down. This restlessness was most unlike him. He pressed his secretary's number.

'Sarah, alert my driver and security. I'm off to Winkfield.'

Chapter Twenty-Four

Following closely behind the leading police car, the Jaguar pulled into the well-known entrance. The security guards were now familiar with both the police escort and the Premier's driver, so banter was the only hazard they encountered. Shaw felt the genie of his tensions loose its grip and he knew he'd made the right decision. Mary wouldn't like it, though, for she enjoyed their rare evenings together. So did he, for that matter, but he had obeyed his prompting and, as on most occasions, it seemed right.

Toby Simpson, upright, handsome and looking very much at ease, was there to greet him. He'd make a great Foreign Secretary when Sir James hung up his boots – but that, of course, was some way in the future.

'Toby, the way you look you wouldn't think that any danger was within a thousand miles!'

'Sir, the Army have three defensive bands around this place. It's like the triple walls of old Constantinople.'

'Does the Captain think we're overdoing it?'

'No, he said that we were rightly careful and that they're grateful.'

'Does he mind being cooped up like this?'

'No, in fact they all seem quite content, and the Captain loves the garden. Bill my driver and he are always chatting about the various plants. He has one routine, though, that seems a little strange.'

'What's that?'

'He climbs on to the roof each morning and evening and stands there very still. It's as if he's listening for something.'

'Have you ever asked him why?'

'No. He'll tell me if and when it's necessary.'

Perfect, Toby, the PM thought. That's exactly the right approach.

'Where's the Captain now?'

'Walking. He usually has a stroll around this time. I've a good idea where he is. Would you like to join him?'

'Perhaps we'd be intruding.'

'No, no, he'd be pleased to see you.'

'We're having a really good summer spell,' Shaw commented as they walked off.

'Yes, Sir, and just enough rain to keep the grass from browning... Ah, there he is!'

＊

'Prime Minister, how good to see you,' the Captain said with obvious warmth. 'You know, I had a little whisper in the mind that you were coming!'

More than a whisper, Toby guessed.

'Captain, when I'm with you I feel I'm with a friend I trust.' The Premier's words were obviously sincere and Toby had to turn away. 'Toby, are you all right?' he added.

'It's all right, Sir, I've caught Sir Winston's bug. I get a little emotional at times. What you said just caught me, that's all.'

'Well, Toby, that's a fairly up-market bug: I wouldn't complain about the inconveniences!'

'Prime Minister...' the Captain began to say, but started chuckling, 'that was a fine riposte!'

'I try,' the Premier shot back. Then all burst out laughing.

'Sir,' the Captain began, when the humour had subsided, 'you're concerned about this latest submarine incursion.'

'I am, Captain. It's a disturbing development. Submarines are not for hire. It's the state-sponsored element that worries me.'

'Well, Sir, we sense no darkness in the vicinity at present, and when we do Toby will know immediately.'

'That's certainly reassuring, but somewhere trouble's being incubated.'

＊

Drusilla Cavendish-Browne's favourite aunt lived on the outskirts of a village in Somerset, halfway between Crewkerne and Montacute. The front of her cottage was secluded by a rather overgrown garden but at the back there was an unimpeded view over rolling farmland. Drusilla had spent many happy holidays at the cottage and she knew the countryside well.

Greenery brushed her Mini on both sides as it nosed up the small driveway to the parking space, and there was her aunt looking as graceful as ever. Age had added a wonderful dignity.

All said that Helen Scott should have married again. She had sacrificed herself unnecessarily. True, her husband had been a fine man and his early death was a tragedy; however, life moved on. Yet Helen Scott had not remarried, but there was no shrine-like corner in the cottage dedicated to her husband's memory, just a simple framed photograph on a table and the name 'Major R.M. Scott M.C.'

Drusilla skipped out of the car and rushed into welcoming arms.

'Aunt, have you had your walk yet?'

'No dear, but you've just driven all the way from London. You must have left very early for it's only ten to nine!'

'I like driving in the early morning, and I had a couple of coffee stops. Anyway, after being cooped up in the car I would welcome some fresh air.'

'Right, let's go!'

They started down the public right-of-way preserved for ramblers. It was a familiar route to Drusilla. It was not long before her aunt began to ply her with questions.

'I'm all ears, Drusilla. I know you've been to Downing Street and I know you're one of the privileged who've been asked to visit Winkfield. You also told me that you were going to a debate at the BBC. Clearly you couldn't say too much on the phone but here, Drusilla, there are no eavesdroppers!'

They had come to a stile and Drusilla stopped before climbing.

'I was completely tongue-tied at Downing Street until I had a glass of bubbly. But every one was very nice and the Prime Minister was just like a friendly grandfather.'

'And what about Toby Simpson, the celebrity of the hour?'

'Well, Aunt, I met him briefly at a party and then I got this phone call. Since then I've been to Downing Street as mentioned, to an invitation-only debate at the British Museum, where I met the Chief Visitor briefly, and again I've been to a BBC debate where Tom Wynter held his own extremely well.'

'I know the Wynters...a nice family.'

'Lizzie's going out with Tom's brother Richard and she's over the moon!'

'And what about Drusilla and Toby?'

'He rings me up. That's about it. He's 24/7, Aunt Helen!'

'One day I'll get used to these terms! Do you like him?'

'Yes, I do like him. I sense a naturally kind man, a good man really, and he's very witty, but apart from the phone we've hardly spoken. When we've met he's always been on duty. There is one thing, though: he's very calm. I didn't sense this when I met him first at the party, but on the last occasion it was so noticeable. The truth is I find him fascinating.'

'Well, are you going to climb that stile?'

'If you'll stop asking questions I might get a chance!'

They both laughed.

They walked on but mostly in silence as the path had narrowed allowing only single file. Suddenly, on turning a corner, they were confronted by a notice: DANGER KEPT OUT.

'Someone doesn't know their spelling or grammar – or both!' Drusilla burst out.

'This is new, for I walked up this very path two days ago!' her aunt reacted. 'Maybe there's a bull,' she added.

'Aunt, the fields are empty on both sides. Oh I wish I had your field glasses!'

'"Kept out"...' Mrs Scott repeated. 'The farmer didn't write that. Oh, I've just remembered, the farmer and his wife are on holiday. They're retired. They're in Devon, I believe, checking out the B&Bs, for they're thinking of starting one themselves.'

'Do you know who's looking after things while they're away?'

'I don't think anyone is. The land's leased out.'

'Aunt Helen, there's something very odd about all this. I'll hang on for a moment. Can you hear that?'

'No dear, my hearing isn't what it used to be.'

'There's kind of muffled thumping. It's metallic but I think it's happening inside a building of some sort. I'll get a little closer, where maybe I'll hear better. Meanwhile you can put the kettle on. I'll only be a minute.'

Half an hour went past. She's taking a long time, her aunt thought anxiously. Another ten minutes went by and in an involuntary way she found herself retracing her steps along the path. Slipping past the 'kept out' sign, she continued gingerly. She stopped, listening intently, but there were no sounds. Then she saw something glistening in the grass at the side of the path.

It was a mobile phone. Was it Drusilla's? In a state of mounting distress she hurried back to her cottage, then, rushing out again she went next door. The son of her neighbour was a wizard with all modern gadgets. He would know if the mobile belonged to Drusilla.

The teenager quickly confirmed Drusilla's number, and, though near to panic, Mrs Scott remembered that her niece could well have Toby Simpson's number on the memory bank.

'*The* Toby Simpson? Wow! There it is, Mrs Scott.'

'Can you phone the number Jimmy please?'

Jimmy didn't answer, but simply pressed the numbers and gave the phone to Mrs Scott. Then he left the room.

'*Simpson here.*'

'Mr Simpson, I'm Helen Scott, Drusilla's aunt. I'm afraid I've awful news. Drusilla's missing! She then proceeded to describe exactly what had happened.

'*Mrs Scott, can you give me both your phone number and address*'

Mrs Scott spelled out the details. Her panic was subsiding.

'*Is there anyone with you, Ma'am?*'

'It's all right Mr Simpson, I'm a soldier's wife.'

'*Well Ma'am, very shortly the police or Army will be with you and almost certainly they will stay close by. I will phone you back.*'

The phone went dead.

After thanking Jimmy, Helen Scott slowly went next door to her cottage. What had promised to be a very pleasant evening had turned out to be a nightmare.

'What should I do, Richard,' she said audibly to the photograph on the table.

'Hold firm, dear, hold firm.' That's exactly what he would have said. Then from nowhere she felt a surge of hope. She looked at the clock. It was seven.

She heard a car draw up, and almost immediately she heard the door-bell. Once more she looked at her husband and then strode firmly to the door. It was the police.

'We are your guard, Mrs Scott. We'll be outside, so sleep well.'

'It'll be a long evening for you. Would you like some tea?'

'That would be very nice, Ma'am.'

'I'll make you a flask as well. Please come in.'

They took their helmets off. They looked like boys, she thought.

'You were very quick.'

'From the top, Ma'am, I mean the very top.'

Chapter Twenty-Five

The Captain showed all the sympathy and concern expected of a civilised and sensitive being but his inner peace was undisturbed. This was very obvious to Toby in his own state of agonised impotence. Suddenly Drusilla was very dear and the thought of her being subject to the whim of some fanatic was maddening.

The SAS had closed in on the farm with their usual skill and stealth but the birds had flown. To where was the burning question, and they had luggage as it were. The little scraps of evidence at the farm had made that obvious. Also Drusilla had heard banging. But how would they transport the stuff and not arouse suspicion in a country area where things unusual were noted? Of course, Toby thought: a tractor and trailer. He went to see the Brigadier immediately and explained his thinking.

'Someone will have thought of it, I'm sure. I hope you don't mind the meddling.'

'Minister, such ideas can be very valuable. I'll pass them on at once.'

'And, Brigadier, knowing the farmer and his wife were on holiday is local knowledge. My guess is that the safe house is in the immediate area.'

The Brigadier said nothing but lifted the phone and dialled the ops HQ near Yeovil. Then he spelled out Toby's message.

'Thanks, Brigadier,' he acknowledged and took his leave.

But where was Drusilla? And who were these people? Were they criminals or fanatics? That he felt was answered easily. Criminals don't hire submarines but fanatics can and do control them. That being the case, what would fanatics do when confronted with an inconvenient snooper? Keep her as a hostage, possibly, but she would be awkward baggage. On the other hand she could be held in a safe house – but the Yeovil area wasn't anonymous London.

The final option made him shudder: cut down by hate-obsessed fanatics brainwashed to believe that their particular mind-set was the only truth. Eliot's words, 'distracted by distraction from distraction', fitted his condition to a tee. He had circled the garden twice this morning and now it was the third. Preoccupied as he was, he didn't hear the Captain approach until he spoke.

'Toby, you're troubled.'

'Yes, Sir, I fear the worst and I feel so impotent!'

'Toby, what if we dress ourselves in soldiers' uniforms and journey to the area of Drusilla's disappearance? No one except the Brigadier and the PM need know. Remember, I can discern the subtle climate, the tensions, the fears, the poison of hatred and, on the other side, those pools of joy and peace. And, what is most important for this mission, I can locate the focus.'

Toby took his mobile out.

'Let's contact Mr Shaw immediately.'

He pressed the speed button and a Downing Street secretary answered at once. Without any preliminaries he asked for the Prime Minister.

'Is it urgent, Mr Simpson, he's in a meeting. Shall I interrupt?'

'Yes, it's urgent!'

'Toby, thank God for your call! It's allowed me to escape from the Chancellor and his economic gurus! They're worried about faltering growth rates. I asked them how long they expected growth rates to continue, for, especially with the new industrial giants, it seemed to me we'd need three planets to sustain us! They laughed politely but I didn't get an answer. Sorry, I'm letting off steam. Our so-called economics does that to me. You were calling!'

Toby explained the Captain's proposals.

'Do it, but get the SAS to be your driver! Good luck!'

The PM hadn't mentioned Drusilla. He didn't need to. Simpson knew that he'd been quite upset.

'We've got the green light, Captain!'

*

Now that he was actually doing something, Toby felt much more at ease.

The Brigadier entered into the spirit of the adventure with vigour but Toby noticed that his treatment of the Captain had become even more respectful. In a sense the Captain was putting himself in harm's way and that was soldier's language. Such was the way of things.

Little time elapsed before Simpson and the Captain were in uniform. Both were privates and both were given weapons, but unloaded. There were no concessions except that the Captain was allowed to wear his tinted glasses. In less than half an hour two Army trucks slipped out of the back exit from the Manor complex. They were on their way and in the company of exceptional men who seemed to be alert and poised to act. Fixed in two rows, facing each other, the seats were anything but comfortable but no one complained – certainly not the Captain, who seemed to be enjoying himself. Toby, though, could have thought of better ways to travel.

'Why did you join the SAS?' The Captain asked the man opposite.

'The challenge, Sir: could I do it? That sort of thing.'

'Breaking down the limits. Does that describe it?'

'Yes Sir.'

'What about the mental limits?'

'Ah, Captain, those are the real limits. You can get hung up on all sorts of things.'

'"Hung up"?' The Captain turned to Toby for an explanation.

'Caught up in, Sir,' Toby answered.

'Hung up's good, I like it!'

'What kind of things do you get hung up about?'

'Thinking I wont be able to keep going. That sort of thing.'

'What about your ideas and beliefs?'

'Captain, I'm only a soldier, not a parson!'

'Isn't "only a soldier" a limit, a kind of hang-up? You're much bigger than that.'

'What am I then?'

'Ah, that *is* a question!'

The powerful soldier was silent for a time. Clearly the question had alerted him. This kind of situation was so typical of the Captain, Toby mused. But he never overdid it. The measure was exact.

'You know, Captain, when I think of it I don't know who I am. They call me Joe Brown and, big deal, I'm in the SAS. But there's more to it than that!'

The Captain smiled but made no comment. There would be ample opportunity at Winkfield.

Then the banter started. The Captain revelled in it, matching joke with joke, but the barbs were those the padre would have sanctioned, a natural respect for the Captain saw to that. Suddenly they were silent, almost stoical in their manner, and after half an hour or so they stopped for tea. An hour later they had lunch, sandwiches in the car park of a service station. Toby had imagined something much more secretive but that, of course, was *Boy's Own* fanciful. No one mentioned Drusilla. They almost certainly knew, but there are things that, being just too close, are left, even by men hard trained in deadly confrontation.

By mid-afternoon they arrived in the western outskirts of Yeovil and, although he was beside the Captain's calming presence, Toby felt his underlying tension heighten.

Chapter Twenty-Six

Ali was in turmoil. He had disobeyed an order; confession would be little less than suicide. He had been told to shoot her, but he couldn't do it: those gentle eyes, so terror-struck, had been too like his elder sister's. He'd fired the handgun into a sack of grain so that they would hear a shot. She was bound and gagged so she couldn't make a noise, but the thought that they might check if he had carried out his orders made him shudder. He almost turned to climb the stairs again to where she was but he couldn't do it. Sheer aversion froze his movements.

He gave the handgun back to his smiling leader – a mocking smile, laughing at his youthful sensitivity. Then they drove off, two on the tractor, two in the trailer and two travelling in an aging Ford behind.

Ali was in the trailer, very aware of the weaponry secreted under farming paraphernalia. He did not know their mission, only the leader and his deputy knew, but he had been told that it was vital and that he'd been exceedingly blest to be chosen. All this had been intoxicating yesterday, but today the world was grey with doubt. Indeed, until he knew he 'couldn't do it' the world had been a simple place where rules were fixed and duty known.

He was the youngest, the one who knew some English and could get the shopping when the safe house hosts were out. They were out tonight, so he knew he'd have to be the shopper. This he didn't mind; it was far, far better than the other menial jobs that he was given. As they approached the house his agony of mind returned with what seemed greater force. All the training from the time he was a child, the learning off by heart, the Mullah's exhortations, all seemed to scream at him that he had greatly sinned. Yet he 'couldn't do it'. That was the certainty in his mind.

When they reached the safe house he was sent off shopping as anticipated. At least here in the supermarket he didn't feel that he was lying. In fact, he bought the food requirement with the practised ease of any shopper and paid cash. While struggling home, festooned with plastic bags, he saw a poster pasted on a vacant shop-front: 'God is Love', it said. It hit him like a hammer and he put his groceries down. So also was the God of Islam, the most merciful and the most compassionate. Was this the reason that he 'couldn't do it'? Was it that simple, love forbade him? The groceries were heavy. Then he thought of the lady trussed up like a chicken. She would not be eating, neither would she be drinking. Dear God, he thought, the misery she must be suffering. He hadn't thought of it before. He left the groceries inside the safe house gate and walked on. This was not a studied move. It simply happened. Just as he 'couldn't do it', he couldn't go inside. How would he get to the farm? He had no idea but he started walking. A hundred yards further on he saw an Army truck parked a little distance up a side road. Automatically he quickened his pace but he felt no fear.

*

Drusilla was desperate and panic rose and fell like waves. Thirst and hunger were growing agonies, but there was so little hope. Who would find her on the meal loft floor so far from easy hearing? She had eased herself snake-like to the door and with her feet had hammered loudly, but only silence was her answer. Hope was difficult to conjure and the nightmare of the sleepless hours ahead, when others were in bed, was horrible to contemplate. At least it was the summer. And she was lucky, very lucky, to be still alive. The teenager that they had sent to end her life had failed to carry out his orders. She had no doubt whatever that she owed her life to him. She also was quite certain that, in sparing her, the boy had put himself in mortal danger, for the other lot, the older men, had sacrificed humanity to their cold, myopic creed.

She heard footsteps. She held her breath. Had they come back, or was it the farmer returned from his holiday? Her heart was thumping and fear rose to possess her. The footsteps now were on the wooden meal-loft stairs: young quick steps. She feared the worst. They had come back and it would soon be over. Resignation brought a sudden calm. She sighed, but tensed again as the bolt was drawn back.

It was the teenager and instinctively she knew that she was safe. The young man said nothing but released her gag.

'Thank you,' she whispered.

Then he undid her hands. He didn't even have a knife. Next her ankles were released. She was free, but her first concern was the 'boy', for that was how she thought of him.

'I couldn't do it!' He blurted out.

'You speak English?' Drusilla reacted.

'Very bad – I speak.'

'Do they know you disobeyed their orders?'

'No! – I run away after I get shopping for them.'

'Where are they?'

'Safe house – Yo-vil.'

'Let's get away from here, they may come back to look for you!'

He shook his head vigorously.

'They no come back, they never do.'

'Where are you going to eat?'

'I got food at shop when I got the shopping. I eat sandwiches on way here. I got lift on trailer, and I have chocolate bars. I stay night here sleep on hay bales and then move on.'

'The Army may come back to scout around!'

'I hide, eh! And tomorrow maybe I get job. England full of jobs!'

Drusilla was still wearing the trousers she had worn on the way from London and in the back pocket there was a slim notepad with a tiny pencil attached. What was more, she had thirty pounds secreted in its pouch. Pulling it out, she wrote down her mobile number.

'What is your name?'

'Ali.'

'Well Ali, if you are in trouble ring this mobile number. My name is Drusilla, and here are thirty pounds to help you on your way. You saved my life, Ali, and I'll be eternally grateful.' Then she kissed him lightly on the forehead, after which she turned and left.

Once outside she began to shake and her legs felt as if they were the creatures of some intoxicated reveller, yet she battled on, but when she got to her aunt's house there was no one there. The key was under the flowerpot as usual so in she went, and straight to the bathroom. There she quickly showered in an almost hyperactive way. She needed to relax … and Toby, she must ring Toby. She sat down on her aunt's favourite chair and suddenly she felt exhausted. 'How stupid!' she exclaimed aloud. She had forgotten to get the safe house address from Ali, but to ask him to betray his own might have been a bridge too far. The phone rang. It was Toby's voice!

'It's Drusilla, Toby, I'm at the cottage.'

'I know, we're at the farm and have picked a young man up who says he knows you. We believe him – he's got your mobile number.'

'He saved my life, Toby!'

'Drusilla, in my eyes he's now a VIP. Just stay put, Drusilla dear. The Captain's with me and we'll be over soon.'

'Toby, I stupidly forgot to ask Ali about the safe house.'

'That's maybe just as well. Anyway, the Captain found it. The darkness was potent, he said.'

Chapter Twenty-Seven

Toby held Drusilla tightly until he felt her agitation calming.

'Drusilla dear, the medics say that you should have a check-up at the hospital,' he whispered softly. He felt her stiffen. 'But I feel you ought to see the Captain first.'

They released their embrace. My God, she is beautiful, Toby thought as he looked at her.

'Not the hospital, Toby. They mean well I know but...' she hesitated, 'I don't know – I just don't want to go! You must think I'm very weak, but I want to sleep in my aunt's familiar bed with the quiet countryside outside. Yet, if you feel I must go, then I must go.'

'No musts Drusilla! Would you see the Captain though?'

Her eyes lit up.

'Oh yes!'

'Methinks I have a rival!'

'Don't be silly, Toby!' She punched him playfully.

He smiled. It was a total giving and he knew without the shadow of a doubt that he was looking at his future wife.

'Where *is* the Captain?'

'He's in the garden talking to your young friend Ali.'

'That will be another transformation!'

'What do you mean, dear?'

'Well you've changed, and Freddie Sharpe!'

'What about Freddie?'

'He was always entertaining, but the last time I saw him on the box he was quite a force. And that announcer Billings – even *I* like him now!'

*

Simpson could see at once that the young Iranian was transformed. The furtive, frightened look was gone.

'You look much better, Ali,' he said easily.

'I no fear, Sir. To live with fear and hate is hard.'

'You are safe now, Ali, and if you want it you will be given asylum. But you will need to be patient, for when it comes to law we move carefully.'

'What about others?'

'They are surrounded. It's up to them.'

'They will choose martyrdom.'

'They're killers, Ali. Martyrdom's for saints!'

'They believe martyrs, Sir.'

'Yes, Ali, they probably do.'

'We will be ever grateful to you, Ali.'

'That what made me know I "couldn't do it", that you grateful too!'

'You're right Ali, love is humanity's companion.'

Toby felt exhausted, but what must the Captain be feeling? His usual routine had been totally disrupted. Quietly leaving Ali in the care of the SAS man who had conversed with the Captain in the truck, he moved out into the garden. He could see the Captain busy in conversation with Drusilla but he could also see that he was weary. This was unusual, but then it had been a most unusual day.

Toby knew he had to intervene and he did not hesitate.

'Sir, you must rest,' he said as firmly as he dared.

'Toby, you're right. I've been rather profligate in spending energy today. Maybe I can lie down somewhere. That would be good.'

Toby, with the aid of Drusilla, saw that the Captain's need was met immediately.

'How long do you require, Sir?'

'Half an hour, Toby. Thank you.'

Drusilla was concerned.

'I hope I didn't overtax him!' she said when they had gone downstairs.

'No, Drusilla; as he says, he's been rather busy – "distilling darkness into light", he calls it! It's a total giving, Drusilla, and his body feels the strain at times.'

'People like Billings changed so radically!'

'The inner cup was fairly full; it just needed a top-up!'

'But, Toby, it's happened more than once: for instance Freddie Sharpe, and now my young saviour, Ali. Look at him, he's smiling from ear to ear.'

'I asked the Captain about this. He smiled and simply said the

118

one intelligence was supreme and everywhere, so I pressed him further. He smiled again and was silent for some time. Indeed, I rather though that I had gone too far. Then he spoke – I'll do my best to paraphrase. The Absolute Intelligence is absolutely intelligent; that intelligence is everywhere and within everything. The same applies to love. So, in this great oneness, like is drawn to like quite naturally yet with great precision, for the intelligence, being absolute, has no limit.'

'Toby, that's powerful stuff. No wonder the Captain was reluctant to be drawn.'

Toby's thoughts quickly conjured up the reaction of the Inquisition and the *fatwa* of the modern era, but he said nothing.

'You've changed, you know!' Drusilla said quietly, turning to him.

'Yes, my ego's much more polished.'

'I'm serious. You've changed.'

'Well, I'm with him every day, Drusilla. My dear, I've been greatly blessed.'

He smiled and kissed her on the cheek.

'You didn't ask me how I felt and if I needed the medics!'

'The answer's written in your look. The tension lines have gone.'

'I don't know how, for all we did was talk about my family. Ah, here's my aunt.'

Mrs Scott was unashamedly emotional as aunt and niece held each other tight for what seemed ages.

'I'm a soldier's wife. I lost my husband, but these things don't get any easier. Thank God you're back!'

'Where have you been?'

'The nice policemen took me shopping.'

Then there were the introductions; the Captain, though, was still upstairs. Toby knew they couldn't linger as the French President was due the next day, but how were they going to get the Captain back to Winkfield? Not that rattling truck again, no way, Toby thought. They needed something to eat, and what were they going to do with Ali? They couldn't leave him unprotected. Quickly he sought out the SAS Major and all at once his troubles seemed to vanish. Everything had already been arranged. The Major also told him that the stand-off in Yeovil continued. There had been no movement whatever from the would-be terrorists inside. However, it was early in the game, he said. The press, of course, were having a field day but Ali's role wasn't known, thank God.

Simpson kept in touch with the Prime Minister throughout but at no time did he sense the sound of harassment. He was as he had always viewed him, four square on the deck!

*

After meeting the Captain, as they called him, Ali knew he trusted 'I couldn't do it'. 'It is like a light,' he said to the man with the strange eyes, and the man had told him that the inner light was his best friend. He was to hold it dear for it was the light of truth. He understood this yet he didn't understand. He knew, though, that he trusted this kind man who'd journeyed from the stars. He liked the lady that he couldn't shoot. Indeed he looked at her with a kind of awe and the tall man by her side called Toby: he was nice and like the Captain in a funny way. Everybody laughed a lot. Mohammad, his leader, never laughed. He almost shuddered. The memory of Mohammad's sneering smile when he thought the lady had been shot was still fresh.

The big soldier that they called the Major told him that his life could be in danger and that he would need protection for a while. But the big man was very kind and Ali trusted him. It had all happened so quickly and it was difficult to take it in. Would he feel the same tomorrow? He felt he would for in a way he'd never been one of them. After the senseless killing of his mother and father in the chaos of a riot, the Guard had been his family. He'd been always dutiful and disciplined and had studied hard and he'd been included in the mission because all assumed that he would do exactly as he was instructed. Being able to speak English was seen as useful, if not vital, to the mission as the rest knew very little, but the main reason for his being included was his apparent blind obedience. Ali had overheard all this when no one had suspected he was listening. He had said nothing and kept it to himself. As was his habit, he stood apart, something forced on him by the brutal circumstances of his parent's death. Ali was not, and never had been, as they thought he was.

*

The Major didn't have to ask the young Iranian much about the mission; Ali told him. He felt barely any loyalty to the men who had treated him like dirt. But the truth was he had little to say as he had been always excluded from their planning. He was the one who bought the cigarettes and groceries and who served the endless coffee rounds. The actual mission was only known to the leader Mohammad and his scientist deputy, the others were not told.

He knew they had a rocket, and a sophisticated one by all accounts, and he knew it had been imported in pieces and suitably disguised, but that problems of assembly delayed them. Mohammad went crazy, shouting and screaming until the safe house owners warned him about the neighbours, and then of course there was the empty farm, with space, and far from prying neighbours. The rest was known. All this was given in Ali's halting English but it was all perfectly understandable.

There was not much to go on; even so, it was amazing what the spooks could glean from very little. The Major was wearing an earpiece with an open line to Yeovil. The long wait was only in its early stages; eventually they would smoke them out.

Three hired Jaguars arrived on the road outside the cottage just as the Captain was descending the stairs. The police had been alerted and the A303 would be cleared as soon as they were ready. The locals wouldn't like it but there it was.

'We're not going to tootle back at thirty,' the Major growled.

Soon afterwards a catering company arrived with three hampers.

'Sorry, gentlemen, we will be eating on the hoof. Our Honourable Guest requires his beauty sleep!'

The Captain laughed loudly with the rest.

The guard at the cottage had been doubled. To Toby this news was reassuring.

Slowly the Jaguars edged through the village. Toby sat back in the seat beside the Captain. All in all it had been quite a day.

Chapter Twenty-Eight

The Iranian Ambassador had not been summoned but had requested a meeting with the Prime Minister. This Bob Shaw had been pleased to grant as it heralded a rational approach to what could prove an embarrassing incident. Shaw had met the Ambassador a number of times and considered him a dignified and cultured man. The request came early in the morning following the stand-off at Yeovil; clearly the adverse publicity was, to say the least, unwelcome. This news had also prompted an outraged reaction from the retired naval man who had spotted the submarine and he no longer felt obliged to hold his peace. So the rumours of six men landing were confirmed.

The meeting with the Iranian Ambassador was fixed for 9.45 in the morning. The Downing Street secitariat apologised for the early hour but the PM was scheduled to meet the French President at Heathrow and escort him to Windsor for lunch with the Queen.

When he arrived, the Ambassador was shown all the courtesies and conducted immediately to the PM's private rooms, where the Prime Minister greeted him warmly.

'Ambassador, how good to see you again. Now, Sir, as you asked for this meeting clearly you have something to say.'

'Prime Minister, we are greatly embarrassed by this illegal and unsanctioned incursion and I wish to disassociate Iran from such criminal behaviour.'

'Sir, we are grateful for your prompt and honest response, and for the courage in standing against militant elements in your society.'

The diplomatic language was obvious but Shaw sensed the Iranians' real desire to distance themselves from the whole affair.

'At the risk of embarrassing you, Sir, we feel that the illegal elements responsible for the current stand-off have powerful friends within your religious leadership.'

'This is a delicate area and we tread softly in the hope that reasonable forces will prevail. But I must assure you that the extreme elements that have violated your sovereignty do not represent the majority of our people. You are holding one of the extremists we believe?'

'How do you know this, Sir?'

'We're told it is common knowledge.'

'You've been misinformed, Ambassador! The only person who would have such information is someone in direct contact with the militants in the safe house, which is at present surrounded. This can be confirmed as all phone calls are being monitored. Indeed, such phone calls point to either panic in the safe house or a very foolish arrogance.'

'Arrogance I feel describes the situation well and, indeed, the contact that I have in mind, but we may be able to exploit this situation and get the five men to surrender. When faced with it, martyrdom may not be to their taste!' The Ambassador's smile was just discernible.'

'By good fortune no blood has been spilled so if Iran Air will take them off our hands the matter will be closed.'

'What about the one that you are holding?'

'The teenager was asked to shoot a woman who had stumbled upon the activities at the farm. He couldn't do it, thank God, so he ran away.' The Prime Minister then went on to tell the Ambassador the full story.

The Ambassador nodded with an air of weary resignation.

'Tell your contact that, if any booby traps are discovered in the safe house, the deal is off. Ambassador, this is not negotiable. It goes without saying that they will have to strip. Our men must not be put in danger from a suicide attempt. Ali, of course, will remain behind. No doubt the militants will use him as a scapegoat, an excuse for failure. You, Sir, have been told the truth.'

'Prime Minister, I am honoured by your trust and the sooner I get working at my end the better.'

'Ambassador, if all the diplomats I've met could match your common sense, the world would be a happier place! Now I've had an idea. When all this blows over, why don't you and I take a trip to Winkfield? You'll find the Captain a remarkable being?'

'Prime Minister, you've triggered a decision, for I feel that this illegal incursion has relieved me of any obligation to balance political sensibilities. It would be a privilege to join you.'

*

After the Ambassador left Shaw telephoned the SAS Major at Yeovil to explain the new situation. Again a quick call to Toby Simpson kept him up to date. Now it was the French President and lunch with the Queen, when he might find a private moment to inform Her Majesty of his morning's work. Fingers crossed, this whole stand-off business could be over soon.

*

The French President and the Prime Minister relaxed into the back seat of the Jaguar. The President had a well-fed look; he was taller than the PM and when he smiled his face inflated from a crumpled state.

'That was a most enjoyable lunch, Prime Minister. The Queen was sparkling and witty!'

'And, another thing, her French was much better than mine!'

'Was that French that you were speaking?'

Shaw chuckled.

'I try, but your manner and your style made me look quite agricultural!'

'Bob, that is an exaggeration!'

'Phillipe, even the word "exaggeration" on your lips sounds romantic!'

The President laughed heartily.

'We make a good double act – don't you think?'

'Yes the *entente cordiale* is up and running. But we claim Aquitaine – you lot pinched it from us!'

'We had to, for you were ruining the wine!'

And so the jollity continued.

'You know, Bob, it's not often people like us get the chance to be ourselves. There's always someone lurking with a notebook or a camera!'

'An occupational hazard they call it!'

'The Manor's close. Security's pretty tight. You don't mind being strip-searched I suppose?'

'Only in the winter!'

They swept past a line of saluting soldiers and went straight to the Manor entrance where Toby Simpson was waiting with the Brigadier and members of his staff, along with the French Ambassador and other prominent citizens.

At the brief ceremony the Captain greeted the President in perfect French and Toby noticed that the Captain's Deputy did the same. Even though he had expected it, the actual demonstration of ability was amazing.

For some time the Captain had asked Toby to sit in on the private interviews and in this case the French Ambassador joined him. The whole interview was conducted in French, which strained Toby's A-level ability considerably; indeed some things he missed completely, but there were a number of points which struck forcibly. The President asked about the nature and size of the civil service in the Captain's country. The answer was predictable yet in a way quite striking too. Local matters were dealt with locally and the centralised service was small and exclusive. Indeed it was considered a great honour to be asked to serve the state. This they did with impartial dedication and in return the state catered generously for their private needs. Toby continued to listen with partial success. However he picked up the Captain's words reasonably well, especially when he talked about the rule of materialism and positivist thought, stressing that it wasn't possible to live by logical reasoning alone as a higher level of awareness was necessary. To Toby, this had 'cat amongst the pigeons' potential. The Captain had also mentioned the French statesman Turgot, but he had no idea what the comments were.

Fascinating but frustrating, Simpson described his experience to the Prime Minister, but doubtless there would be a translation.

*

The Prime Minister had checked twice with the SAS Major but there were still no signs of movement. The stand-off continued. Nerves would be stretched to screaming point in the small semi, for bitter divisions were inevitable. Why, Shaw wondered, did men create such hell for themselves?

Chapter Twenty-Nine

The stand-off continued and it didn't take too much imagination to conjure the desperate situation in the semi. Meanwhile local pressure was building up as, naturally, people wanted to go home. So very soon the SAS would have to smoke them out. For Toby the uncertainty was a nagging presence in his mind. Drusilla was still at her aunt's and, although she was completely safe, she was still in the vicinity. What if there were other terrorist elements in the area? What if...? What if...? There was no end to such thinking, he told himself. In any case, one of the best anti-terrorist forces in the world was guarding her.

Simpson had been concerned when he'd heard about the terrorist ally at the embassy and quizzed the PM on the matter.

'I'm glad you think it's singular, Toby,' the Premier had reacted cynically. 'I trust the Ambassador; as for the rest, I'll treat them as a wise man should and keep my powder dry.'

And so the brief and hurried conversation ended. Later he learned from the Brigadier that the secret service boys had had a field day. Initially the leader of the terrorists had been very careless on his mobile. Now it was the opposite, but the Ambassador had confirmed that they had received the PM's offer and had fully understood it. Notwithstanding all this, Toby was uneasy.

The Captain picked this up during their early morning walk.

'You have done all you can, and your Prime Minister has gone as far as he can to avoid bloodshed. Now leave it to the one intelligence. No one can reap what has not been sown. True, the prodigal son turned, but *he* had to turn. The father could not do it for him.'

As usual in such situations, the Captain said no more. But Toby had noticed something different in the last few days. Somehow he was much more forthcoming, much more ready to give advice. Before he had waited; now he spoke as if he were instructing. Suddenly Toby seemed to freeze.

126

'What is it, Toby?'

The Captain had sensed it immediately.

'You will not always be here, Sir. Someday you'll return to your homeland and I dread the day.'

'This physical world is measured by distance, but the mind and spirit have their being in a different medium.' The Captain smiled. 'I'll be closer than you think.' Again there was the smile, but with a mischievous sparkle.

Toby's mobile bleeped.

'Simpson.'

Get Bill to bring you in: I need your support in Cabinet this afternoon.

'Yes, Prime Minister.'

*

It was a full Cabinet. Both the Foreign and the Northern Ireland Secretaries were there. In fact all the Prime Minister's firm support was present. Something was afoot. They had fifteen minutes before they were due to assemble, so Toby went to the loo, always a wise precaution. Unexpectedly he bumped into Tom Wynter.

'My God, Tom, you haven't demeaned yourself and joined the Cabinet?!'

'Nothing so grand, I've just had a meeting with the PM, and I was supposed to be in a meeting in a House of Commons committee room five minutes ago. So I must dash. We must get together!'

Toby smiled. Tom was in the fast lane and driving hard.

'How's the celebrity?' the NI Secretary quipped.

'Got a cramp signing autographs. Got a cure?'

'Don't sign!'

It certainly was a full Cabinet. The room was crowded and slowly they were taking their seats. The Chancellor was already in place, busy with the detail of his voluminous paperwork. Exactly on time the Prime Minister took his seat, but he didn't start the meeting immediately. Instead he seemed momentarily to be reflective. Then he lifted his head and looked straight at the Chancellor.

'You pressed me to call this meeting, Sir, as you are concerned about the economic warning signs. The floor is yours!'

'Thank you, Prime Minister. Well, ladies and gentlemen,

inflationary pressures are worrying, especially with the latest round of wage demands from the public sector. These must be resisted for they are both unrealistic and irresponsible in the current climate. Unfortunately employers are caving in on every side. We have already put up interest rates by a quarter of one per cent and I will propose a further hike this Thursday. Indeed, if things don't get better I will propose a major rise, for we simply cannot allow inflation to take hold. Again I must warn you that VAT increases have not been ruled out! They can be a strong corrective measure. I am of course counting on your support in this matter. Indeed strong unified support from the Cabinet is essential.'

'Chancellor, we are lucky to have your undoubted experience and skill at this time. You have warned us about VAT but this, I'm told, falls heaviest on the lower paid. Tax I know is already at crippling levels. Indeed employers need to find double the take-home pay when employing staff. The statistics are quite shocking. In fact, it is little wonder that our marginal industries have been decimated. Then there's telephone outsourcing which, to put it mildly, is not a favourite with the public.'

'Prime Minister, this is a common feature in modern sophisticated societies. It's simply how things are organised.'

'Yes, George, but is it the only way, or is there a real third way we haven't explored?'

'Prime Minister, we employ the best minds.'

'This we would expect; but Chancellor, these experts write learned papers, and they all have published books: one might say they have a vested interest in the system. No old pro likes being told he's got it wrong.' The Prime Minister smiled and most assumed the old pro was the Chancellor.

'I saw Tom Wynter in the hall, and if it's his ideas that you have in mind, Prime Minister, well I'm afraid our findings show that they're quite impractical.'

'Prime Minister, may I say something?' Simpson felt he had to speak.

The PM nodded.

'I had the good fortune of listening to the economics TV debate live and I can tell you that Tom Wynter held his own. In fact the economics experts made a rather poor showing and one of them was a Treasury official.'

'How embarrassing!' the Chancellor quipped. The old pro had slipped the net.

'Toby, you see the Captain almost every day. You must have picked up the essence of this system?'

'The striking thing about it all is its simplicity. Earnings are not taxed, that is a key factor. In other words, what a man earns he keeps. On the other hand location value, which is created by the community's presence, belongs to the community. So instead of the shop owner paying ground rent to a landlord he pays it to the community. He would have to buy or rent the building, for buildings are the result of human enterprise. Of course the problem of inflated house prices that is causing so much trouble is not due to the building, which needs constant maintenance, but to location value.'

'But, Sir, this is all right for a primitive society, but in a society like ours with leaseholds, sub-leaseholds and sub-sub-leaseholds, location value becomes almost impossible to calculate!' the Chancellor protested.

'I think you'll find Tom Wynter has a model that copes with this. As to the type of society: simple maybe, but not primitive!'

'Thanks, Toby', the PM acknowledged. 'I think we should get Tom Wynter in and then we can ask him all the awkward questions face to face.'

The Chancellor's allies had kept their heads down, Toby thought. No doubt they sensed the way that things were running. Anyway the PM had the majority, there was no point in getting into his bad books when no advantage could be gained.

'Well, Chancellor, for the present we're stuck with the system as it is. But I'm sure that in the not-so-distant future you'll find the challenge of a different system stimulating!'

How Toby kept a straight face was a miracle, but he did. Then the PM released him. Duties at Winkfield were pressing, he explained.

Simpson was immediately beckoned when he left the Cabinet room.

'Minister, there have been developments at Yeovil. One of the terrorists tried to escape but one of his friends sprayed him with a burst of automatic. Amazingly he survived and is now in intensive care.'

'Does the PM know?'

'Yes, he has an earpiece. He gave this note to the Cabinet Secretary.'

One glance was enough.

'The deal is off,' it said.

Chapter Thirty

After Ali's near celebrity status at Mrs Scott's cottage, when he had met the Captain and so many other people, he was taken to an Army camp where, the day following, he was gently questioned. The truth was Ali knew little. He had been a kind of dog's body and a dedicated and unquestioning believer who always did as he was told. Clearly that was why he'd been included: as a useful foot soldier to relieve the others of the menial work. However, the SAS Major was taking no chances. Would Ali revert to type? This was a consideration that made him order a close monitoring of the youth's behaviour. He was not to be held a prisoner but would be placed under a sort of house arrest, so that he could be protected from his former friends and allies. Not that the inmates of the semi could do much; it was their friends who were the danger, for there was little doubt that Ali was the scapegoat for the failure of the mission.

Ali didn't revert. Indeed all he seemed to be interested in was learning English and seeing the Captain again. Visiting Winkfield, though, was a decision for the Minister, Toby Simpson.

The SAS Major, of course, had more immediate concerns. He had learned from the wounded terrorist that the semi was full of explosives. At first he had thought it the warning of a penitent, but he was soon disabused. In fact the terrorist was gloating over the possible devastation and loss of life, especially amongst the soldiery. Indeed, he took delight in saying that the lethal cocktail could be triggered by a mobile phone. The Major looked at him lying helpless in intensive care. He had been riddled with the bullets of his friends, but he didn't blame them; on the contrary, he blamed his own cowardice. Their reaction had been necessary justice. There was courage there, but how perverted by unreason. Young lives were being ruined by a hate-filled creed. The Major was as hard-bitten as any, but now and then it got to him.

Could he believe this helpless man? Why had the young Iranian wired up with drip-feeds told him about the mobile when electronic jamming was routine? But then, with umpteen bullet wounds and drugs to match, his thinking would be anything but clear. Still, the Iranian could take a bitter satisfaction in such falsity. Nothing was certain, yet somewhere between audacity and prudence lay the answer – with one proviso: that the safety of his men was paramount.

The Major had studied the semi from all angles. He suspected that the chimney was blocked; most were. There were no hostages involved so sheer firepower was an option, but it could be messy, indeed very messy if the wounded terrorist's boasts were correct. He needed a neat solution with an intelligence bonus, like laptops not destroyed and, the icing on the cake, live terrorists to question. Smoking them out was his preferred solution, but how to deliver the cocktail was the question. The garden gate was open and the path to the front door was unblocked. Of course! The little robot they were playing with at Hereford. It could be the postman. It was as quiet as a mouse, but would they see it, especially with the street lights on? And switching off the street lights would alert them. It was a long shot but worth a try. Let them stew for another few days. The leader was a chain-smoker, Ali had informed him, and all the cigarettes he had were those that Ali bought the day he ran away. By now the terrorist leader would be out, or near to running out. This and the pressure of the hour would be unmerciful. Yes, a few more days could swing the balance.

*

Stories of division in the Cabinet were now a near obsessonal topic in the press. Sources close to the Treasury and Cabinet Ministers spilled confidences almost on a daily basis. Some headlines were totally irresponsible: 'Our Capitalist system under Alien threat' and 'Alien's culture to be forced on us' were typical. Someone, the PM thought, was working very hard to block reform. He was not surprised, and it was so easy to manipulate the owners of the patchwork holdings of suburbia. Had no one told them that a site location duty would see a corresponding reduction in local tax, and death duties would also be cut, if not abolished? Indeed nothing much would change for the ordinary house dweller. No one was advocating a 100% tax. It would need an age of enlightenment for that, but what was desperately needed was an easing of the pressure. The land on which all enterprise took place was the gift of Nature to all of human kind. To allow a lawful pillage of this common gift was, to say the very least, unwise, for here was the seedbed of unrest: the landless dispossessed. Shaw sighed, thinking of the Chinese sage Mencius. 'Truth', he insisted, 'issued before its time is always dangerous.' Such sayings were a rightful caution but never a shackle, Shaw reflected. Great issues needed men of similar dimension. This was certainly true, but he, Bob Shaw, had a secret weapon: the Captain.

✳

Toby Simpson was again at Winkfield, where the flow of visitors continued unabated. This never seemed to weary the Captain as his day was measured, rounded as it were. Toby hadn't thought to mention age and the natural spans of life but, as often with the Captain on their frequent walks, the question simply arose.

'Our life span is longer than you experience here. Indeed our year is slightly longer. So in Earth years we live on average about 120 years; a few manage 150. But, as you know, Toby, length of life alone holds little value. It's how we use the gift that matters. As it says in your scriptures, we should always keep our hand to the plough, but gently!' He smiled. 'The Supreme is not coerced!'

'Our frantic lifestyle cannot help, Sir.'

'No, Toby, but adversity is useful, for then we realise our frailty and bow to that ever gracious intelligence and love.'

Suddenly Toby said it; he certainly hadn't planned to say it, but then spontaneity seemed to be the rule when in the Captain's company.

'Captain, Drusilla and I would like your blessing. We're going to be married.'

'Toby, this is good news but not exactly unexpected, for seeing you together was to see the future, and Toby, to seek your blessing in the One will keep you one. Excellent news, this calls for a little celebration this evening; perhaps that patient man the Brigadier could join us?'

'Of course, Sir.'

'A little wine on such occasions is permitted!' The twinkle in the Captain's eye was so very natural. 'When does the lovely lady hope to visit Winkfield?'

'As soon as the siege at Yeovil is over; she doesn't want to leave her aunt while the trouble's unresolved.'

133

'A thoughtful sentiment.'

'Sir, to change the subject, we're expecting the three Prime Ministers of Australia, Canada and New Zealand by the end of the week and the Queen will be joining us when they're here. Britain fondly thinks of this as a family occasion!'

The Captain chuckled.

Chapter Thirty-One

Toby Simpson's driver Bill had little to do at times, but he always had to be on call. Often he pottered about the garden and, because he was in many ways an expert, the gardeners didn't mind, in fact they welcomed the help. During his frequent walks the Captain often stopped and chatted about the various shrubs and flowers that he was tending. On one occasion Bill had asserted that gardens were always on the move. Nothing was ever static. 'In the winter months there's not much happening – but there's always something,' he had added.

'Ah, Heraclitus,' the Captain had said mildly and Bill had asked him what the strange word meant. He was told that Heraclitus was an ancient philosopher who maintained that everything was in flux. 'You can't step twice into the same river,' is a way it was described.

'Well put,' Bill had reacted, and the Captain chuckled.

All this Bill relayed to Toby Simpson on their way to his constituency, where Toby had an early morning meeting.

'Bill, you have something more to tell me, I suspect.'

'I asked my son to look up the name Heraclitus on the Net and now *he's* interested!'

'Did you tell the Captain?'

'Yes, he just laughed. Then he added like a kind of throwaway: "Why stop at Heraclitus?"'

'And?'

'Well, that was all, Minister.'

'Bill, when we're together like this you can call me Toby. It would make me feel more human!'

'No, Minister, that wouldn't be right, but thank you for saying it!'

'All right, Bill, but what have you done about not stopping at Mr Heraclitus?'

'My wayward, sixteen-year-old son came up with Plotinus.'

'My God, Bill, that's a good choice. Did he say why?'

'He said he liked the blurb on the Net.'

'Have you told the Captain yet?'

'No.'

'Tell him! – It's amazing: the Captain says one casual word and you remember. Then you tell your son and he gets enthusiastic. Tell me, is the music still as loud?'

'No, he's toned it down.'

'Well, it'll be interesting to know what he makes of Plotinus.'

'Minister, he's already told me of three great principles: the Good, the Intellect and the Soul – just like the Christian Trinity, he says. Where he's got that from I've no idea for I've never seen him lift a Bible.'

'Well, well ... Now Bill, to practical things. This morning's meeting will be short, about an hour I'd say. Then I'd better show my face at the "rooms". There's nothing like a session at a constituency "surgery" to nail your feet to the ground. After that a light lunch; then we're off to Windsor to meet the Queen's officials regarding her visit to Winkfield. And, Bill, you haven't forgotten about tomorrow?'

'No Sir, you're reporting to the House.'

'And on Friday we stay put, for that's the big day when the PMs arrive. And then there's Yeovil!' He said no more. The options and the dangers were well known.

*

Toby's statement to the House was matter-of-fact and brief. The list of callers at Winkfield, he said, was long and impressive. Wallowing idly in luxury was not the Visitors' mode of living. Security, of course, remained a priority and was emphasised by the present stand-off at Yeovil. The fixation of obsessive people with access to sophisticated weaponry was a modern sickness. Poverty was often cited as the cause but the well-fed faces of well-educated youths were often counted in the terrorists' ranks. The cause, he suggested, had deeper roots. Indeed, it felt as if hatred had been nurtured and encouraged. By whom? was the question. They were the real dark souls!

Toby then went on to praise the Captain and his friends for their kindness and understanding. Very few, if any, of their callers left unimpressed. Then he personally thanked the Captain for the wisdom he so willingly imparted. It had to be emphasised that the Captain seldom ventured his opinion until asked – that is, unless in very special circumstances. 'These beings, or human beings I would call them, have developed their faculties to a remarkable degree and we are privileged to be their hosts.'

Simpson then reported on the successful visit of the French President. They were also looking forward to receiving the Prime Ministers of Australia, Canada and New Zealand, when the Queen herself would be presiding. The Prince of Wales and the Duchess of Cornwall also hoped to be present. They were expected back very soon from their tour of the United States and Canada. So Friday promised to be memorable.

The report completed, Simpson took his seat and awaited questions.

The first question centred on the Visitors' habits and how they occupied their day. Did they write things down, and what was their script like?

Toby rose, he felt quite calm, as if he were amongst a group of proven friends.

'Mr Speaker, the Honourable Gentleman has asked a most interesting question. All I can say is that taking notes and writing is not something that they generally practice. They seem to totally trust their memory and, judging by the books that flow from both the British Library and the London Library, there is a lot to memorise. I remember one day I casually asked the Captain to jot something down for me otherwise I'd forget and he did so in a very pleasing script. English, of course. I have never seen an example of their own native script, if I may use the term. Honourable Members, our guests have a massive mental capacity. I would say, though, that they do respect our scientific knowledge and the wisdom of our world's great teachers and philosophers; these they read avidly and I feel they view their stay as an opportunity to study. As for sight-seeing – well, they had a look around before they showed themselves!'

The next questioner followed immediately.

'I have listened to the Right Honourable Gentleman's words carefully but I still think there's something more to the visit of these beings. I am certain that they're peaceful in intent, and these fears of invasion that are still mooted are nonsense, but I feel strongly that there's something else, something yet to be understood.'

'Has the Honourable Gentleman been to Winkfield?'

'Yes, I visited some time ago with a group of MPs.'

'Oh yes, I remember. Sorry, my memory isn't quite up to the standard of our Visitors! Would you mind telling me what your main impression was?'

'Of course. First of all, I *was* impressed. He was so ordinary yet extraordinary in an unobtrusive way. Let's put it this way: when the world seems grey, he would be the man to see. And another thing: I felt that he gave me total attention and I mean total.'

'Mr Speaker, I believe the Honourable Gentleman has answered his own question, for what he has just described is the common experience. The Captain uplifts, and he enlightens. It seems to me to be an inner work. How far the ripples of this work proceed is the question. This I suggest may be the "something else" to which the Honourable Gentleman has referred. One thing is certain, the Captain's work is not merely a vote of thanks!'

The next speaker was clearly agitated.

'I never thought that I would hear such sentimental hogwash in this Chamber. I'm sorry, Mr Speaker, but it's what I feel. A few conversations at Winkfield are not going to change the world. No way!'

Toby was about to reply when he saw Freddie Sharpe's mop of hair bob into prominence.

'Mr Speaker, what the Honourable Gentleman has just said *is* hogwash. He hasn't met the Captain but I have a number of times. He's changed me and if I get the chance *I* will change the world!' At that Freddie took his seat and laughter exploded on both sides of the house.

The next questioner had a ponderous style and a reputation for being an economic expert.

'Mr Speaker, will the Minister inform us why this persistent interference in our economic affairs is tolerated? It seems to me that we're being assailed on all sides by a naïve theory that was dismissed a century ago. All major economists are united on this. Why are they being ignored?'

Toby smiled. He looked as he was, completely unperturbed.

'Mr Speaker, the Honourable Gentleman's assertion of persistent interference – no doubt he means from Winkfield – is incorrect. The Captain only answers questions and he never interferes. There is no question of him endeavouring to influence policy. When it comes to naïve theory the Honourable Gentleman is entitled to voice his opinion, but there are many who might equally question the taxation theories now in place. Certainly, if simplicity were the badge of truth, they would find it difficult to qualify. I am not an economist, but the theory that location value is created by the community as a whole makes sense, indeed it is self-evident. My friends tell me that the principle is simple: the community takes what the community creates and the individual keeps what he creates – that is, the product of his labour. Today we do the opposite. Which proposition is naïve? That is the question.'

Toby sat down and another somewhat agitated member rose.

'Mr Speaker, planning restrictions hike the price of land. It's so obvious: release these smothering restrictions and the price of property would even out. Why does nobody see it? Why are we wasting time on this unworkable theory?'

Simpson stood up, not knowing what to say, but words came just when needed.

'Mr Speaker, planning will always be necessary in a community but such planning should accord with the natural sensibilities of the community and not a sectional commercial will. The central site is the central site, and here planning is largely a practical and aesthetic matter. Indeed planning, by its very nature, is a secondary factor, for without the primary factor of location no planning is possible. It is true that planning permission can bring huge capital windfalls, but this again is due to location. Planning is the enabler in such cases, yet what is enabled can differ considerably with location. Of course, in truth, the capital value belongs to the community, for the community as a whole makes this value possible; in fact, with our present system, this golden egg is rather like winning the lottery. However, if the community received what it created and the individual his full untaxed earnings, the problem would largely be eliminated. Indeed, if location value were collected by the community, planning permission would enrich the community fund.'

The debate was drawing to a close and, after three more brief questions, the opposition spokesman rose slowly to his feet. In rounded tones he thanked the Minister for his care and diligence, while pledging his support. No mention was made of the Yeovil stand-off; that was rightly considered an Army matter. Again there was no reference to any of the Ministerial answers. Of course, much of the opposition had come from the government benches. He'd got away with it, Toby thought. There was another thing: no one, thank God, had asked him when the Visitors were leaving, for so far it was a question he had studiously ignored.

With a practised blend of casualness and precision, the Speaker concluded the debate. Toby lingered on the front bench until, as expected, Freddie Sharpe slipped across. Then they walked out together.

*

The rush-hour traffic was lighter than usual, so the journey to Winkfield was easier than expected.

'You've had a busy day, Bill,' Simpson said when he'd finished his phone calls.

'Not as busy as you Minister! How did the debate go? I couldn't get it on the radio. Must have pressed the wrong button.'

'All right but not memorable – that sums it up, I think! You know, Bill, I don't seem to get worked up any more. I was as cool as a cucumber today. It can only be the Captain's influence, for like you I see him every day.'

'My wife tells me that I'm easier to live with, so something's getting through!'

Simpson chuckled.

The phone rang. It was Drusilla.

'Drusilla dear, it's nice to hear your voice. All's well down there I hope.'

'Yes, I'm taking my aunt to North Devon tomorrow, so I'll be driving back to London soon.'

'When are you coming down to Winkfield?'

'When you ask me!'

'Drusilla, it's an open invitation. Captain's orders!'

'Toby, you were so cool and calm today. I was proud of you.'

'I'm lapping up the praise. Wasn't Freddie fun!'

'Brilliant! Listen, I tried to get you at Winkfield but everybody there seemed to be in a tizzy. The Prince apparently arrived out of the blue and he and the Captain are already like old pals. He only flew in this morning!'

'That's the Prince! Well, we'll be seeing him soon for we're off the motorway and heading for Windsor. So when will I see *you?*'

'*I can't be certain until I'm sure my aunt is settled in, but it will be soon.*'

They chatted on until the Winkfield entrance was in sight.

'You're a lucky man, Minister,' Bill said bluntly when Toby put the phone back in its holder.

'I am, Bill. Very much so.'

Chapter Thirty-Two

At the entrance they learned that the Prince had already left. They must have passed him on the way. It was odd, though, that they'd missed him; but, of course, a low profile was good security.

At the Manor Simpson found everybody gathered round the television. The reason was soon apparent. The siege had ended with predictable suicidal violence. Toby sensed at once that the commentator knew little, so he went at once to find the Brigadier who, unusually for him, was in his office.

'Ah, Minister,' he greeted, 'take a seat. I'm just off the phone with the Major. He's exhausted but very much relieved that his men are OK. The SAS are human, so it seems! Seriously, it went well, they bagged them all and, except for one, the medics think they'll all pull through.'

'Who's the one?'

'The owner of the safe house.'

'That's a pity for he must know a thing or two!'

'Minister, sometimes these cells are very tight.'

'What about the leader Ali mentioned?'

'They had to strap him down for he was completely mad, biting and punching with his one good arm; the other one took two bullets. A chain smoker without fags for maybe days ... add to that the tension of the siege. What's more, these guys can't grab the bottle!'

Toby nodded.

'What about the house? Wasn't it supposed to be wired up?'

'The experts are going through it inch by inch. They found one laptop but they've taken it away to be opened in a safe place, whatever that may mean.'

'The laptop could be useful!'

'Very, if we're lucky.'

'Strange they didn't wreck it,' Toby pressed

'That's why they're being extra careful; these nutters can be very clever! And, Minister, I'd almost forgotten: Ali wants to see the Captain.'

'That can be arranged. How could we deny Drusilla's saviour?'

'The Major's quite taken with him, I believe. But I fear the young man could be in grave danger for, when the terrorists eventually have access to lawyers, they'll blame it all on Ali. That's what the world will hear!'

'Surely it's all *sub judice*?'

'It should be!'

'Anyway, thank God it's over.'

'Don't say it! With these guys it's never over. We must not drop our guard.'

'Alas, you're all too right.

Toby looked casually about him. The Brigadier's office was Spartan. There was a wooden desk, a wooden chair, a phone, a filing cabinet and a laptop, mostly for incoming e-mails, Toby guessed. The Brigadier was not the e-mail type.

Simpson got to his feet.

'Well, Sir, I'd better report to the Captain.'

'The Prince was here earlier, and was with the Captain for over an hour, I'd say. They spent most of the time in the garden and they both looked very much at ease. Of course, the Captain always does.'

*

Toby knocked and opened the door to the Chief Visitor's study-cum-drawing-room. The Captain was sitting behind his desk as usual, but he wasn't reading. Indeed, he seemed to be reflecting on something.

'Ah, Toby, you've had a busy day for I saw you on the box, as you call it. You were most impressive. And our mutual friend Freddie, well that was a masterly intervention. Now, Toby, I upstaged you for I've had tea with the Prince. What a charming man. He has invited me to Highgrove. Would security allow the adventure?'

'Well, Sir, if both you and the Prince desire this, it would be difficult for us to stand against you.'

'But if you did?'

'Then the custom is you would obey, for it would be assumed that our decision was in your best interest.'

'Excellent, no wonder this nation has survived so many tests!'

'Captain, apart from being unusually calm, I had a rather strange experience as I walked into the Chamber this afternoon: I suddenly saw this being, Toby Simpson, as a stranger, a dream-like figure taking its seat before the despatch box. But Sir, I was very quickly back with Toby Simpson!'

'Toby, remember what your great poet said: "We are such stuff as dreams are made on, and our little life is rounded with a sleep."'

'My heavens, we did that for the school play and I thought that Shakespeare was just playing with words!'

'Such men mean exactly what they say.'

'But, Captain, who was watching?'

'You were.'

Simpson shook his head. How could the answer be so simple?

'Toby, when the great teachers talk of One they mean exactly that. The witness, present in us, is not locked in a box.'

'Sir, I think I need a little time on this one!'

'Yes, a little reflection can be useful.'

'Sir, I've just remembered, young Ali wants to see you.'

'When can we fit him in?'

'Most days except Friday.'

'Toby, you decide. And what about your beautiful lady?'

'Drusilla's taking her aunt to North Devon, so it will be a few days before she's here.'

The Chief Visitor and the Minister with special duties sat in silence for some time. In fact it had grown to be kind of custom. Toby felt no awkwardness and he liked the peace. Busyness could be pursued at other times. Presently his mind was focused on his experience at the despatch box and the question, who was watching? He closed his eyes and for no apparent reason images of the garden filled his mind. The memory of the trees was vivid. Their presence seemed to thrust itself at him. Then it struck him. They're watching! *Their* presence is a watching.

He spoke of this immediately and the Captain looked at him like some indulgent father.

'When Master Teachers such as Plato emphasise the One, they mean exactly what they say. You're right, the presence is the watching, but there is One watching; there is no multiplicity of witness.'

Toby was speechless; the Captain's words had hammered home, but understanding them in practice was a lifetime's work.

144

Chapter Thirty-Three

The terrorists had failed on three occasions yet the surge of electronic chatter pointed to a fourth attempt. Winkfield on Friday was a perfect target but security was watertight, so what could they do? Such scares the PM had to deal with all too frequently and with the available facts before him judgements had to be made. For Friday all that could be done had been done; that was Simpson's judgement. It was time for trust, yet he felt uneasy. However, the Major was arriving soon with Ali so he could always 'bend his ear' a little.

*

Even though Ali was accompanied by the Major, he received a full security check at the entrance. This the young man didn't seem to mind. He trusted the Major and so he trusted all of those the Major trusted.

They left the car at the entrance and walked towards the Manor and on the way were greeted warmly by Toby Simpson, who escorted them to the Manor and the Captain's presence. Ali was overwhelmed and, even though the Major had warned him that less than friendly people walked the streets, the kindness that he'd met had left its mark. In the past he'd grown to believe the people in the West were wicked, but what he had experienced was the opposite.

Ali was a handsome young man, lean and of average height. His naturally innocent nature had been ruthlessly exploited. Now that innocence was tempered by experience and a newborn confidence in its own perception. Ali was maturing.

Tears welled up when Ali saw the Captain. He was just the same, he thought, or rather knew, for the sameness was not anything outward, like his face and smile; the sameness was somewhere behind those quiet eyes.

'Your English is improving, Ali,' the Captain responded to Ali's greeting.

'It still not ... sorry ... It is still not very good, Sir,' Ali said slowly.

'Practice makes perfect, Ali!'

Ali repeated the aphorism twice in an effort to remember.

'But some people practice bad things and they do not become perfect! Ah, maybe they become perfect at bad things? Is that possible, Sir?'

The Captain chuckled.

'Very good question, Ali. The dictionary describes "perfect" as faultless. So if you were perfectly bad, would you be faultless?'

'The opposite, Sir!'

'Well Ali, you have your answer.'

'Oh, I like this talking!' the young man reacted.

'So what are your plans, Ali?'

'I do not know, Sir, but I want to know what is right and what is true, for I have been told many things.' Ali spoke slowly, picking his words carefully from memory.

'You remember, "I couldn't do it"?'

'I will never forget it, Sir!'

'Well, Ali, that inner light ...'

'Yes Sir, it was a light!'

'Then remember that and wait upon it.'

'I think I understand, Sir.'

'You will,' the Captain said quietly and in some strange way Ali knew he would.

'I haven't been to Mosque, for the Major is worried some fanatic might guess my person. But I don't want to go. Young men my age get angry and excited over silly things. I used to get excited too, but I tired of that. Sorry, I am tired of that. I like peace I find with you.'

'Ali, have you ever visited a shrine of the Sufi tradition?'

'I do not know, Sir, but once I entered the inner room of a holy place and I burst into tears. I will never forget, Sir. It was very wonderful, very peaceful – like being with you, Sir.'

'Yes Ali, there are reports of such a place. Did you linger long?'

'I did, Sir. I did not want to leave, but the old Dervish attendant coughed, and I knew I had to go.'

The Major, who was sitting in at the side of the room, was enthralled, for Ali had revealed himself in a wholly unexpected way; but it was the Captain who had drawn him out. What had impressed the Major most was the total absence of reaction on the Captain's face when his presence was equated with the stillness of the shrine. Such humility was rare.

The conversation had then taken a lighter turn, but one wholly appropriate, and now the Captain was suggesting a walk. Again, it was just right. Indeed, it seemed as if his actions harmonised with all around quite naturally.

*

The intelligence briefs landing on the PM's desk made for troubled reading. All the experts felt that some major 'gesture' would be staged to shock the nation and divert attention from the 'family' gathering at Winkfield. It was all too feasible and the usually unflappable Shaw was disturbed. He had already pestered the overstretched security services, but they, of course, were very much aware and, indeed, they had been pestering him! All he could do was pray. All? His attitude, suddenly seen, shocked him. Had prayer descended to a last resort, the final option of the arrogant mind?

Shaw was sitting in the deserted Cabinet room. He often retreated there to do some thinking, as he put it. His hands, stretched out in front of him, were flat on the surface of the table. Impulsively he turned and lifted the phone on the table behind him.

'Prime Minister,' an efficient sounding voice said instantly.

'Susan, how did you know I was here?'

'We always know where you are, Sir!'

'That's more than I do!' Shaw quipped. 'Could you get me Canterbury, please? I mean the Archbishop!'

'Yes, Prime Minister.'

Shaw didn't expect a quick reply, but within three minutes the phone rang.

'The Archbishop of Canterbury for you, Sir.'

'Thank you, Susan.'

'James, are you very busy today?'

'No, Bob, I have a light day. Is there something I can do?'

Both men had known each other since they were boys.

'It just struck me a few moments ago that in this sophisticated age we pray as a last resort and it shocked me. So I thought that we ought to make a gesture of praying together not at a grand ceremony but at some simple service. The nation needs a lead, a plain, simple example. James, I'm concerned about the

147

current situation. Security-wise we have done all we can and I'm turning to an old friend. The humility to bend the knee is what is needed!

'Well, Bob, you're in luck, for I'm dedicating a small church in Kennington that's just been renovated. But there isn't much time. I'm due there in an hour.'

'I'll be there. Give me the address.'

Shaw wrote the details on the note pad.

'Better still, Bob, come to Lambeth Palace and we'll go together. Will Mary be coming?'

'No, she's on her way back from our daughter's place in the country.'

'I'll see you soon.'

*

It was by chance that Simpson pressed the remote. At first he saw the familiar figure of the Archbishop of Canterbury addressing what was a very small congregation and thanking the hard work of dedicated members in some recent renovations: a very typical English scene, but why was it being televised?

'My God!' he burst out. There was the PM, as large as life, sitting in the front row with his security man. What was going on? Then his attention switched back to the Archbishop, who had clearly moved on to wider subjects and the recent spate of bomb scares.

'Today we find ourselves under attack by extremists whose murderous creed wreaks random carnage on the unsuspecting. Uncovering these violent beings is difficult for a tolerant society used to freedom of movement; even with such provocation we must not stoop to ape their ways, yet we must be vigilant for in our vigilance is our safety. Many have suffered sorely from this intolerant madness, while many have escaped miraculously when devilish devices failed to activate. Our security forces deserve the support of all. Their job is far from easy and an error on their part is easily magnified. Remember this: God is wholly compassionate; God is Love; he is not a God of random killing.

'I would urge us all, regardless of our religious persuasion, to stop sometime today and let our busy thoughts subside. Give thanks for the gift of life and the wonder of creation. Ask for strength to be a servant of the good. That is all, for something quite forbids another word.'

Simpson watched, transfixed. This wasn't the usual Church approach, and by heavens it was powerful. He continued to watch as the Archbishop left the pulpit and took his seat beside the Prime Minister. Then they prayed together. The visual image said it all. How many were watching? he wondered. There would be repeats, for the media would not be able to resist it. Then Toby remembered and he himself sat down and closed his eyes.

*

Toby knocked gently on the Captain's door and entered. The television was on and Simpson saw that it was channel one. He was about to speak but stopped for the Captain was sitting very still, his eyes half closed as if on the point of sleep.

'I'm sorry, Sir,' Toby muttered and made to leave.

'Toby, it's all right, I was obeying the Archbishop.'

'You look pleased, Sir.'

'Some deeds echo through the ages, especially those that seem to happen.'

Chapter Thirty-Four

The Archbishop's secretary had never seen so many e-mails, and there had been numerous letters delivered at the gate. Again the BBC and ITV were pressing for interviews. Then, of course, there were the phone calls from the Bishops, and his personal friends. The sudden avalanche was just too much and the exhausted churchman was by necessity forced to rest. Indeed, his wife, well aware of his Friday obligations, made sure that 'the Archbishop is resting' was heeded.

*

Winkfield was crowded; they had tried to restrict the numbers but it had proved impossible. Security seemed little more than nominal as the guests began to arrive. Cars, though, were checked thoroughly and most decided to walk the modest distance to the Manor. The Queen arrived precisely on time at three o'clock, followed by the Commonwealth Prime Ministers who had earlier lunched with her at Windsor. Their cars, having been inside the Castle wall, went straight to the Manor where the Captain, the Prime Minister, his wife and the Minister Toby Simpson were waiting at the front of the house.

The Queen greeted the Captain first and he gently bowed his head in a gesture of respect. As usual Toby Simpson was fascinated for the gesture was so natural; indeed, as he had always noticed, the Captain played his part with easy grace. Considering that the Queen performed this type of function endlessly, her words and those of the Duke were remarkably fresh. Next the Prime Ministers were introduced to the Chief Visitor; Toby didn't hear the words but, judging by the laughter, the right note had been struck.

The Queen stayed much longer than scheduled. Simpson saw her busy in conversation with the Archbishop; no doubt the subject was the previous day's broadcast. Indeed, there were few who didn't hear the familiar voice address them, including Simpson himself.

'Mr Simpson, my husband says that you're running a rival establishment here and ought to be incarcerated in the Tower!' the voice said with mock severity.

'I hope the cells are *en suite* Ma'am!'

A gust of laughter united them.

'I believe the Indian Premier is arriving next week,' the Queen continued when the humour had subsided.

'Yes Ma'am, followed by the Italian Premier and the German Chancellor; then the Brazilian President. And the Irish will be here on Monday, but of course it's their second visit. They were greatly impressed on the first occasion. It was quiet for a time and now it's rather busy.'

'As I said,' the Duke cut in, 'a rival establishment!'

There was another ripple of laughter.

'When's the Russian President coming?'

'In a fortnight's time, Ma'am.'

'Thank you, Mr Simpson.'

Toby bowed and the Royal couple moved on; now they were busy in conversation with the girl clearing away the tea things that had been set up earlier. Here was the magic of monarchy. It was a moment the girl would doubtless remember for the rest of her life.

∗

The Prime Minister had contrived to retreat inside the Manor with the Captain. 'Standing around', as it were, had never been his favourite occupation, and in this the Queen's stamina always amazed him.

'I hope you don't mind me saying so, but you look rather anxious today.'

'I am anxious, for the intelligence landing on my desk lately has been very worrying. I was convinced they would do something today, but so far nothing, thank heavens!'

They sat in silence for some time.

'What you and the Archbishop did yesterday was a powerful example, Sir, and I rather had the sense you hadn't planned it,' the Captain said quietly.

'You're right, Captain.' Shaw then went on to describe what had happened.

'The event was repeatedly presented on News 24. Many people would have watched and I rather feel that many would have copied you. Such a general stilling of the mind works well beneath the outer show. Prime Minister, violence lives by violence and its sister, agitation; it shies away from peace.'

'Are you trying to tell me that our simple act of praying in a small, near-empty church has had an effect?'

'Prime Minister, we cannot know what happens, but sometimes, it would appear, we are the instruments of transforming power. This is something that we cannot order and should never claim.'

*

Formal meetings between the Commonwealth Prime Ministers and the Captain were due to start at four-thirty and hopefully would finish not long after six. Then they were off to Downing Street, the guests of the Shaws: a private affair, Bob Shaw emphasised, without any frills.

*

Not long after the Australian PM went in to see the Captain, Simpson found himself with free time on his hands. All day, from the moment he got up, there had been details needing his attention, now there was a window. But not for long, as it was just then that Freddie Sharpe decided to phone.

'Toby, did you listen to the radio this morning?'

'Freddie, I haven't had time to breathe!'

'Well you missed real entertainment!'

'Put me out of my agony!'

'Jim Billing firing on all cylinders – it was brilliant!'

'Who was the victim?'

'Well, the Editor of one of the heavies was stupid enough to let 'Archbishop of Fairyland' head a scathing article on the event at Kennington. Billing called the Editor in and I suppose he expected a pat on the back from a fellow member of the chattering class. He was shredded! Billing tore him to pieces, but in the most polite way – and that made it even more telling. The Editor got ratty, which didn't help him, and snapped, "Prove the existence of God!" But Billing was masterly, replying that a full ontological explanation would take some time. "You know, Joe," he said, "it's a bit like asking you to prove you had a father!" Anyway, the Editor had the grace to laugh.'

'Thanks for letting me know, Freddie. The Archbishop was

152

here today but I didn't hear a word about this. We were and are somewhat preoccupied. Well, it seems that Jim Billing has changed. Period, as they say. The Captain wants to see his special friends more often, he says. That's you and Jim and a few others, so hopefully we'll be seeing you soon.'

'Just give me the nod and I'll be down like a shot!'

Toby walked out into the garden, stretching himself. Suddenly he remembered that he hadn't checked his voice mail. Thankfully there was only one call. It was Drusilla; she was on the way from Devon and hoped to stay the night with family friends at Virginia Water. She could come to Winkfield tomorrow.

Chapter Thirty-Five

When Drusilla turned into the entrance at Winkfield, she was much earlier than expected, so Toby wasn't there to welcome her. Everyone knew who she was, of course, for one look was enough to impress the dullest observer. Security, however, had to be observed and, while she herself was waved through, her car was subjected to the usual rigorous inspection.

Suddenly the apologetic attitude of the soldiers transformed.

'Run, Ma'am, run,' the Sergeant barked. 'Corporal, escort the lady to the Manor.'

'What's wrong?' Drusilla asked the Corporal breathlessly.

'We found a device under your car.'

'Who would have put it there?'

'That's the big one, Miss!'

The Corporal's brisk pace kept her voice strained and breathy. She felt shocked and vulnerable, and the horror of the farm ordeal was reborn. Then she thought of the very real danger the soldiers were facing at the entrance.

'What about the men at the gate?'

'They'll call up the experts. We've got three of them here.'

'Still, it's very dangerous!'

'Yes Miss, these things are never a piece of cake.'

'And you're going back there – putting yourself "in harm's way", they call it. It feels very real.'

'Yes Miss, it's very real for the bomb disposal guys. Bloody heroes the lot of them! But Miss, you had it tough at the farm. That was as bad as it gets!'

'Yes, I still have nightmares, I'm afraid.'

'Ah, there's the Minister. I'll leave you now, Miss.'

'Thank you, Corporal.'

They converged quickly, running into each other's arms.

'Oh Toby, thank God you're here!'

Simpson sensed her real distress at once.

'This on top of the other. My worst fear is not being able to cope,' she continued, her voice muffled against his chest.

'You'll cope.'

'But they must be following me!'

'I doubt it, dear, you drive too fast! No, they must have planted a tracker somewhere on your car.'

'I see, I never thought of that.'

'They probably fitted the explosives at Virginia Water. It was all too easy, the bleeper would have called them in. Drusilla, the main thing is, you're safe. This place is ringed with soldiers. In fact, my dear, you're more secure than Downing Street!'

'Toby, you're an old smoothie! You're trying to calm me down!'

'Drusilla you *are* secure. My secretary's suite is quite generous, so she'll be able to put you up, but one thing is certain, you can't go home tonight and there's no appeal!'

'Dictator!' she reacted playfully.

After Toby had left Drusilla in the care of his secretary, he phoned Downing Street and left a message for the Prime Minister; then he went to find the Brigadier who, as he expected, was with his men. They were inspecting the car and clearly treating the situation with great respect.

The Brigadier was quick to escort Toby well away from the scene.

'It's a mobile-phone-triggered contraption – clever, well thought out, the lads say, but fitted in a hurry. They're waiting on some more equipment, but they're near to certain the signal failed.'

'How would they know to set it off?'

'Someone following in a car, or maybe a micro-camera super-glued to the car somewhere. I'm not an expert, Sir.'

'Well, if you're not an expert, I certainly don't take the prize. But the blessing is Drusilla's safe.'

'What a beautiful lady, and doesn't she dress well? Modesty itself: she leaves all those half-clad women in the shade. You're a lucky chap, Minister.'

'Brigadier, the name is Toby. I think we've known each other long enough!'

'Bernard will do, Sir.'

'With a name like that, the next step must be Field Marshal!'

They laughed.

'It seems almost indecent to laugh, knowing the dangers current at the gate.'

'Toby, laughter is present even in the direst situations. I've seen it! It's the oil of humanity!'

Just then Simpson's mobile bleeped.

'Yes, Prime Minister.'

'Thanks for your message and thank God Drusilla's safe! There's also been a car bomb attempt up North but it didn't come off.'

'Probably meant to coincide with the one here. The Gods are on our side, Sir.'

'Toby, at one time I would have assumed that that was a figure of speech, now I'm not so sure! I'm thinking of coming down tomorrow. What's the best time?'

'Lunchtime, for the Prince is coming in the morning and in the afternoon the Captain has asked to see some of his special friends, such as Freddie, Jim Billing, young Ali and my driver's son. I think he wants to see them on a regular basis. You and the Archbishop, of course, are high on his Richter scale! That is if he has one! In fact he doesn't have favourites but he can discern an open heart or one that's in the throes!'

'Toby, while I'm on ... I need you at the Cabinet meeting on Tuesday. The Chancellor has academia on his side and he's bringing one of the big guns to lecture us. I've asked Tom Wynter. No doubt you can guess the rest!' Laughter crackled through the handset. *'It's difficult to decide who despises me the most, the economists or the "God is dead" brigade!'*

'Well, Sir, the terrorists and their apologists are not too far behind!'

'Alas, they're a running sore. But, turning to positive things, Toby, I would like to see the Captain at an Oxford or a Cambridge College. You know, fielding questions from a panel of reasonable men!'

'Perhaps you can sound him out tomorrow, Sir.'

Toby smiled to himself. The PM had got the bit between his teeth.

'The Captain is a blessing. We must give him every opportunity to speak, for I fear he may be leaving us much sooner than we think.'

'Yes, Sir.'

'See you tomorrow.'

The Brigadier, who had moved out of earshot, turned again towards Simpson.

'That was the PM. He'll be here for lunch tomorrow,' Toby responded. 'Apparently there's been a bomb attempt up North, but thank God it was a damp squib.'

'Amen to that!'

At that the two men went their separate ways, the Brigadier briefly to the gate; he didn't want to crowd the men too much. Toby strode off to find Drusilla, for he feared the shock she had sustained would not dissolve too easily. Of course, with the Captain present, she was in the best possible company. God! The very thought of her being the victim of some mindless fanatic was difficult even to contemplate, yet this had been the fate of many. The madness of it all was infuriating. Anger and hatred, though, solved nothing. They merely added fuel to the fire.

Chapter Thirty-Six

The Prime Minister, with the full knowledge of the Iranian Ambassador, had called in the fierce-eyed Shia cleric whose conciliatory behaviour had helped to calm an awkward moment at the British Museum forum. His suggested task was to interview the six terrorists being held in the secure wing of a Hammersmith hospital.

The medical costs, not to mention the security requirements, had been enormous and the PM was impatient to deport them. The safe house owner, who had been a Syrian asylum-seeker, was not a British citizen. The other five, including the one who had lost his nerve and been mown down by his friends, had been questioned repeatedly, but little had been gleaned. However, the laptop abandoned carelessly at the safe house was a treasure trove. Strangely, it was the one who had lost his nerve who proved to be the most belligerent, yet he in his panic had also left his mobile intact. This again was a treasure trove, though none of the numbers matched that used in the failed attempt on Drusilla's Mini. Things were rarely quite so neat.

Shaw found the Shia cleric taciturn and enigmatic. He was unmistakably a Shia but one of independent mind, and bluntly honest. He had no time for what he termed the 'idiot thinking' of the ignorant. Shaw liked his directness. When he told the cleric what he intended, the fierce eyes burrowed into the floor before him for what seemed ages.

Eventually he lifted his head.

'Yes, I will see them.' The brevity was eccentric.

'When I met the Captain last, he quoted Latin, which in itself is remarkable, but then the Captain is remarkable,' Shaw said, hoping to initiate a conversation.

'He is.'

'"*Si vis amari ama*" is the quotation, and the meaning, according to the Captain, is: "If you want to be loved, love!" So, Sir, we have given these men the best of medical care and are sending them back to their homeland. We have questioned them but not harried them and are hoping that humanity may arise to modify their hatred.'

The cleric stood up.

'Thank you for your wisdom, Prime Minister, I will do as you wish.'

Then the he his leave and left quickly.

'Well,' Shaw muttered, 'there goes brevity's disciple!'

He lifted the phone.

'Yes, Prime Minister.'

'Sarah, I need the car in fifteen minutes, if you please. It's Winkfield.'

*

Toby Simpson met the Prime Minister at the entrance and together they peered inside the tent erected while forensic activities were proceeding on Drusilla's car. They had found the tracker and the micro-camera, but Toby said that they had volunteered no further information.

'They're certainly painstaking, Sir, but how long can we go on like this. It's is the fourth attempt. I see no end to it, and now I feel Drusilla needs protection – and, by God, the press make sure of that!'

'Toby, the tabloid mentality survives because we buy the tabloids. It's the same with the questionable music that we're bombarded with. It's the democratic will, and that no one dares challenge – so they think. We need a great man, Toby, someone who embodies principle. Let's walk to the hall, I want as much time with the Captain as I can.'

For a time they walked in silence.

'By the way, Toby, keep Tuesday free. I need you in Cabinet; it's the economic debate with Tom Wynter and the Chancellor's expert.'

'I feel that George will battle to the end!'

'He's a mainstream economics man and he thinks his reputation is in question. Yes, he'll dig in all right. I wish he'd throw away his academic righteousness, but George is George! To change the subject, I assume Drusilla's still here?'

'Yes, Sir.'

'Best she stays for a little while. I feel sure she wasn't the target initially, just the means of delivery, but, as you've said,

159

with all this tabloid coverage it's a different story. How do they get this information with security as tight as it is?'

'A snippet here, a snippet there: then two and two make six. In other words they pad it out a bit.'

'How can we encourage integrity?'

'Sir, what you and the Archbishop did is still reverberating. I've heard that some City companies are setting "quiet" rooms aside.'

'But will it help integrity?'

'Well, Sir, people need to "stop and stare" *occasionally*. There's little point in reasoning with a headless chicken!'

Shaw laughed, and once again they lapsed into silence.

'We're almost there, Toby. How long have I got?'

'The afternoon people are coming at 2.30.'

'Good, that gives me well over an hour. When did the Prince leave?'

'About an hour before you came.'

'We're not overtaxing the Captain I hope?'

'I don't think so. He would tell me if we were. Yeovil tired him, but then there were pretty negative forces present.'

*

The fierce-eyed cleric did visit the terrorists in their 'fortress' ward, where he found their attitude full of posturing. He told them this quite brutally in his own staccato way, but he did not criticise their mission. They had to recognise the pointlessness themselves. Following this, he spoke to them each in turn, but it was the leader who had been weaned off cigarettes that most surprised him, for what he found in him was mildness. However, bitterness and hatred still burned in the one who had tried to escape. The cleric, with his usual brusqueness, told him he was only covering up the shame of weakness with a trumped-up show. This was too much for the enraged extremist, who suddenly struck out wildly with a table knife he had secreted on his person.

The terrorist leader soon overcame him, but the cleric had been injured; not badly though, for the knife was blunt. Surprisingly, the incident did not reach the press.

Despite all this the PM was still intent on deportation. But what would happen when they touched down in Iran? That was yet to be revealed. Would they be heroes, would they face disgrace or would they simply be ignored?

Chapter Thirty-Seven

The Cabinet room was buzzing with pre-meeting chatter. Everyone was in place, including Tom Wynter and the Chancellor's academic choice, a rotund man very much at ease and confident. Tom Wynter, Toby judged, was rather like a greyhound in the slips.

The Prime Minister called the meeting to order and began by welcoming Mr William Smyth, the well-known economist and broadcaster, and Mr Tom Wynter, now also a familiar face on our TV screens. First they would each present their case, with Mr Wynter focusing on the place of location value in our tax-collection system. Afterwards there would be ample time for questions. Mr Smyth would speak first.

The Chancellor was smiling confidently and, establishing eye contact with his cronies, assured that his man would carry the day.

Smyth rose, adjusted his papers, and began what was a persuasive and erudite outline of the main planks of government policy, of which control of inflation was the priority. Next was the need to moderate public-sector wage pressure. It was impressive and there was little doubt of Smyth's mastery of what was often horrendously complicated. Indeed he didn't put a foot wrong and sat down to general nods of appreciation.

Wynter was next; his rather lean, boyish appearance seemed out of place, yet the Prime Minister had invited him as the best spokesman in support of the system outlined by the Captain. He began by acknowledging the wisdom and mastery of the previous speaker, but his next sentence, 'This, however, is not the whole story,' set the scene. And from then on he cited example after example where community projects, financed by public funds, gave massive windfall gains to private interests. He outlined the tax imposts that forced businesses to out-source abroad. The use of the self-employed in the corporate workforce was all part of the same pressure. All this, he emphasised, was

161

inevitable given the current economic model. Then he said, with obvious understatement, that the world stock exchange system was misguided. Saddling a company with a perpetual debt was questionable. Clearly all Wynter's points were meant to stimulate debate, but he was at pains to emphasise that any instant application of economic reform, as he saw it, needed the care and wisdom of such men as William Smyth. There could be no overnight change of any major proportion. Our current system was enormously complicated and unpicking it was not an easy task. Again there were general nods of approval and Toby made quite sure he caught Tom's eye.

The Prime Minister was fulsome in his appreciation of both presentations. Then he called for a break of fifteen minutes, before questions.

Simpson made no effort to contact Tom Wynter as he was surrounded. Instead he sought out the PM, who was on his own and watching the scene, while the Chancellor was invisible behind the wall of his supporters. Could it be that the Chancellor had been working overtime and had the Cabinet sewn up? And if so could the PM pull the rabbit out of the hat?

After the break the first question was directed at William Smyth.

'Can you see any possibility of a land impost in our present sophisticated society?'

The question said it all. A plant, Toby guessed.

Smyth was quick to answer.

'Frankly no; for one thing, the leasehold complications in the City and, indeed, the high street, with all the contractual ties, would be baffling. The time required to implement any significant change would be considerable and would allow the next government to repeal the tax before it was properly applied. And I don't need to remind you gentlemen of the political difficulties, especially with our property owning society. The average householder sees his property as one that is house, garage, if he has one, and garden. To have different tax systems for the land factor and the house would excite instant opposition. If fact, it would be seen as an unnecessary complication. Aren't things complicated enough? they'd say! Just imagine the appeals the council would receive on their assessments!'

'Mr Wynter,' the Prime Minister prompted.

'I agree with Mr Smyth that there will be difficulties – initially – but these difficulties will become secondary once we understand the simple principles which are at the heart of the reform.

'The average householder, as you say, will regard his house, garage and garden as one property, but this description leaves out one element, possibly the most valuable element in that property: the land it all stands on. The value attributable to the house etc depends on their state of repair; in other words, the value depends on the effort of the owner. The land value, however, is entirely dependent on location. A fine distinction, you may think, but quite near where I live a rather attractive detached house once stood in a generous garden; now there are five town houses on the site. Personally I preferred the former building. My point is that the owners of the property had no difficulty in differentiating between the land value and the building, and quite honestly I can't see this causing a comprehension problem in the suburbs.

'The location-value charge is not just another tax the Chancellor may apply. It should be seen as a shift from taxing human labour and production to the collection of a value created by the community as a whole. As has been said many times, the community would take what it creates, i.e. community value, and leave or considerably reduce the impost on human enterprise. I would emphasise again that this represents a shift in tax and is not simply another tax imposed on the overtaxed citizen.

'A very old friend said once that "government will do anything for you except get off your back". The aim is to substantially ease that burden!'

'Mr Smyth?'

'I have listened with interest to Mr Wynter; all I would say is that, in the area of application, the difficulties are primary, not secondary.'

'Thank you, Mr Smyth. Next question,' the Premier called.

Simpson took the opportunity.

'Mr Wynter, being in the Captain's company frequently I've become a fan of the location-value system. This you know, but in trying to explain the measure I've been confronted with a kind of automatic resistance. A common reaction is: this is land nationalisation – the Communists tried it! How do I counter this?'

'The land is not taxed, for it belongs to no one. It's the value created by the community that is collected, hence location value. Land nationalisation is an historical mindset, which in my opinion is wholly misleading. We are not advocating a national freeholding of all the island's land. We are merely the custodians.'

'Idealistic stuff,' an elderly member reacted.

'Without the ideal, there is nothing for the practical to refer to.'

'Mr Smyth?'

'Again, I am listening with interest. I liked your last statement Mr Wynter – excellent!'

Simpson could not help but see the scowling features of the Chancellor. Clearly the incumbent of Number Eleven had not expected Smyth's conciliatory attitude. Toby smiled. 'The best-laid schemes o' mice an' men gang aft a-gley.' Burns had scored again.

'What naïve rubbish!' a voice boomed out. Toby smiled. This again wouldn't help the Chancellor for the Minister for Sport was known for his Churchillian habits but not his tact. 'We should have a pulpit, for it's more like a prayer meeting than an economics debate. Freddie Sharpe was right that day: we're all too bloody selfish to put this to the test!'

Toby expected the PM to knock him down, but he merely chuckled.

'Well, Mr Wynter?'

'The Minister for Sport has raised an important point, indeed a fundamental one. Self-interest is natural but I have observed that those who only think in selfish terms often come unstuck. Serve your client well, go that extra mile, and he will note it and be loyal. It pains me when I hear of healthy companies ravaged by asset-stripping predators in a ruthless quest for gain, a gain that is often the capital value of the freehold site or sites. In my view, this is inexcusable. Of course, if the community received a substantial slice of location value, this temptation would be considerably reduced.'

Questions continued, but Toby knew the high point of the meeting had passed. The Chancellor wisely kept his powder dry and his cohorts took his lead. The key had been William Smyth.

He, as it were, had come prepared to scorn but had remained to pray and this had swung the meeting.

The Prime Minister was clearly pleased, but he was careful to include the Chancellor in his summing up. Conciliation had always been Bob Shaw's preferred approach.

Chapter Thirty-Eight

Toby gave Tom Wynter a lift to the station and was thus able to glean the jist of the *après*-meeting conversations. Apparently the PM had been very complimentary but had also made quite of fuss of William Smyth.

'I'm not surprised, Tom, for I've never seen an academic bow so gracefully before a contrary argument.'

'We're going to have lunch at his club. The Chancellor was party to Smyth's offer but I got the feeling that the Chancellor didn't like it much.'

'Tom, George was sidelined, that was the long and short of of it. And his sycophantic followers will drop him like a hot coal when they see he can't deliver.'

'Will he fight back?'

'With what? Ah, here we are at Waterloo. Will we be seeing you on Sunday?'

'*Deo volente.*'

'See you then.'

'Bill, it's Winkfield,' Toby said, sitting back in his seat.

'Right, Sir.'

'Your boy coming on Sunday, all right?'

'Try and keep him away! You wont believe this, Sir, but he wants to be a vicar?'

'What sort?'

'C of E, that's what I put on my Army form. He used to go to services when I was in the regiment.'

'Is this something he talked about?'

'No, never said a word. Can't imagine anyone less churchy!'

'Canterbury, here we come!'

Bill laughed, but Toby knew that he was hugely pleased.

The phone rang.

'Yes, Simpson here.'

'*Go by the back way, Sir. We've just been very lucky.*' Toby recognised the voice, it was the Sergeant at the entrance. '*We've just escaped a suicide attempt. The Deputy happened to be here at the crucial time and froze her in her tracks. We were very lucky. A powerful man is the Deputy.'*

'Well, he *is* Deputy to the Captain! Thanks for the call, Sergeant.'

'Bill, there's been a suicide-bomb attempt at the entrance. We've been told to go the back way.'

'What are these bods on about?'

'Winkfield is the prime publicity target.'

'For what?'

'We'll soon know for predictably the bomber will be "helping the police with their enquiries". But I doubt we'll hear much. Such unfortunates are the foot soldiers, the useful idiots of their "betters"... that is, if it's who we think it is.'

'And if it is, why attack the Captain and his friends? What have they done?'

'They chose a heathen country to settle in, or they simply don't fit the mind-set. Bill, the truth is, I don't know!'

'What do you mean by "the mind-set"?'

'In this instance, an exclusive belief system married to passionate tribalism; the terrorist is enslaved by its dictates, just like a prisoner by a ball and chain!'

Bill was quiet for a time as he negotiated the roads towards the back entrance.

'But we've all got mind-sets, Sir!'

'Yes, and they can bind us tightly too!'

'I've never thought of it like that, but you're right, we're all kind of lost in our own world and the half time we miss the obvious, but does this let the terrorist off the hook?'

'The good book says, "According to their deeds, he will repay." So things could get pretty rough for some. Of course, this works both ways, for instance young Ali knew he "couldn't do it". It was like a light, he said, but he obeyed – and what a payment!'

'What was that light, Sir?'

'The light of humanity. Bill, why don't you ask the Captain about these things? This is second-hand stuff I'm dishing out!'

'Not bad for a charity shop, Sir!'

Toby burst out laughing.

*

Bill delivered Simpson right to the door of the Manor, where they parted with the usual shot of banter.

'Bill, don't forget to follow up your questions with the Captain. The charity shop has its limits!'

The big ex-Army man chuckled and then walked off to the room he had been allocated. God, he had been lucky to land such a job. Clearly his Army CV had helped, but what pleased him most was his son. The boy had been transformed. It was the Captain, of course; he was simply remarkable, not only for what he said, but for what he was, for peace seemed to be his very substance.

After resting for ten minutes or so, Bill headed for the garden and there was the Captain, completely on his own. It was not his usual time for walking but immediately he saw Bill he headed in his direction. At once the conversation centred on gardening and continued on the subject for some time. Eventually there was a lapse and Bill, hesitant for a moment, described his conversation with the Minister.

It was obvious to Bill that what he had reported had greatly pleased the Captain – indeed, like some event he had been hoping for.

'So what is you question, Bill?' the Captain prompted.

'Sir, what is the light of humanity?'

'It's your inner light, the gift of our Absolute Father in whose image we are made. This is the message of the wise. The light shines everywhere but it can be grossly covered by the crust of habit.'

'Thank you, Sir.'

The Captain smiled.

'Bill, young Bill is doing well, very well indeed.'

Tears welled up but emotion was controlled.

Chapter Thirty-Nine

The Brigadier thought he had seen it all, but the baby-faced young girl quite prepared to throw her life away had caught him on the raw. The Deputy had spent a long time with her and had said with confidence that she had a new perspective. Even though she was the human bomb, primed to kill and maim his men, the seasoned soldier felt sorry for her. Indeed to him she was simply the pawn of a cruel will.

They were on the way to take her to be questioned. These were the rules, but he would speak for her; at least that was something he could do.

The Brigadier had experienced many postings but Winkfield beat them all. The endless VIP visits and the hyper-security was one thing, but it was the sheer goodness that radiated from the Captain and his Deputy that was unique. The Minister Toby Simpson had been imbued with this same quality – almost all remarked upon it. Something very special was happening here, but then journeying from a distant planet was special, especially when it was beyond the solar system.

'Sir,' the Sergeant called from the door of the wooden hut erected as a shelter at the entrance, 'they're about ten minutes away.'

'Ring the Manor, the Deputy might want to see her off.' He could say an extra word of encouragement, the Brigadier mused. Idly he paced up and down, then involuntarily he turned towards the Manor, and there was the Deputy already on his way. My God, what if the convoy coming for the girl were to be hijacked? The Deputy would be in the front line. Was he being paranoid? Maybe, but he couldn't ignore the impulse. He barked a few orders and extra security manifested in minutes.

'Hold back, Sir, until I give you the all-clear,' he said quietly as the Deputy came up beside him.

He could hear the trucks drawing up on the road outside. The high hedge made them invisible. Judging by the laughter, all was well, but this was interrupted by the high-pitched ranting of a woman's voice. Immediately the Brigadier went to investigate and found a woman remonstrating in a near hysteria. She was a lawyer. No one had the right to search her. Then she saw the Deputy at least ten yards away and she stopped, transfixed, her screaming swallowed by the sudden silence.

'Who is that?' she whispered. 'He's standing in a pool of light.'

'Our honoured Visitor, the Deputy.'

'Unbelievable, and we've been told he is the enemy of our faith. We've been misled, our faith betrayed, for all I see is goodness.' The Brigadier turned to look but he did not see what she was seeing. One thing, though, the agitation that had been troubling him had vanished.

'You still need to be searched, Ma'am,' the Brigadier said quietly.

'Of course.'

She was a striking woman now that her ire had cooled, aristocratic in her features, Somalian maybe.

Everything had been transformed. The lawyer, having thrown away her brittle arrogance, was tending to the young bewildered girl with natural tenderness. Thank God, humanity had triumphed, prompted by that amazing being, the Deputy. But where was he? The Brigadier scanned the scene. He'd vanished.

Everyone had tea in mugs passed round by the soldiers, and of course the Brigadier was handed one. He smiled; the men always made good tea, and in the most amazing places. He remembered the tight spots he'd been in.

'Look after her, Ma'am. She's an innocent,' the Brigadier said firmly, singling out the lawyer.

'I will, Sir,' the lawyer said with equal strength. 'Brigadier, I've learned a lot today! Would that I had learned it earlier. I only wish I could express my gratitude. That's my one regret.'

'It's all right, Ma'am; I will pass it on.'

*

Simpson learned of the drama at the entrance from the Deputy and was assured by him that all was now 'at rest'. The Captain's number two was a commanding presence but Toby had often noted how respectful his behaviour was in all his dealings with his chief.

'He is held in the highest esteem at home,' he once confided, 'and when the Chief Elder chose him as mission leader no one was surprised.'

At the time Simpson was very tempted to probe, but he let the matter pass. Such questions, he felt, were best asked of the Captain.

Being assured that all was well at the entrance, Toby sought Drusilla and found her with his secretary, helping with the Sunday arrangements. Even though the guests generally had e-mail, Toby wanted all to be confirmed by phone. This was not a routine gathering, Toby sensed; he felt sure the Captain had something important to impart. He hoped it wasn't what he thought it was, but he feared it was. If they were returning it had to be for some good reason, for the few weeks they had been here (that is, assuming their undeclared period was small) hardly justified such a journey. Yet their view of time could well be different. Real presence, as obvious in the Captain and his Deputy, was timeless.

'While you've been enjoying yourself in London, we've been very busy!' Drusilla quipped. 'How did Tom get on?'

'Very well indeed, even his supposed opponent was complementary.'

'Good for Tom! He knows he's coming on Sunday, I hope?'

'He does.'

'Well, we've sent him an e-mail anyway.'

'Have they all been contacted?'

'We can't contact the New Zealand newsman as yet. But that's the only one.'

'The King of Brevity, as the PM calls him, has he accepted?'

'Yes, the fierce-eyed cleric will be watching us.'

'And Ali?'

'I spoke to the Major myself. He'll be here. I hope Bill and his son will be coming all right.'

'Try and keep them away! Freddie and Jim Billing, of course, are part of the furniture. And there's Tim Bates.'

'They e-mailed back almost immediately.'

'Oh, Minister,' the Secretary interjected, 'there have been urgent phone calls from Oxford about the Friday dinner at Balliol.'

'Has Cambridge invaded?'

'They were very anxious to speak to you, Sir.'

'I suspect it's security; the secret service have been told to pull all the stops out and they'll be doing just that. The whole thing's a nightmare, but there it is, the Captain is going to Balliol. Anyway, we've always carried on regardless. Being British, they call it! Some might think of other names but I prefer the original! Well, I'd better phone them, I suppose!'

Toby went directly to his office, pleased at how well Drusilla was adapting. Her car was ready now, but she did not seem to be in any hurry to leave. Anyway, there was little point with Sunday coming up. The atmosphere at Winkfield was special and, given her terrifying experiences, it was the best possible place for her to be. Simpson sighed, what a lucky so-and-so he was, and her vulnerability made her even more attractive. Then it suddenly struck him: had they forgotten his sister? He scribbled Lizzie on his pad and then slowly but resolutely he lifted the phone.

Chapter Forty

The scene at Balliol was classic. On the high table was the Master, flanked by the Prime Minister and the Captain, and on either side were the Deputy and Toby Simpson, while from the walls the commanding gaze of Curzon and the witness of the red-robed Harold Macmillan were companions. It was quite a setting, the PM mused. The Master rose, scanning the tables laid out in their customary rows. He began, emphasising expansively the honour that they felt in hosting such an historical event.

'You will notice that we have placed the Chancellors of Oxford and Cambridge at opposite ends of the high table; that, of course, is for security reasons!' There was an immediate surge of laughter, as all the guests had been subjected to rigorous security checks. 'In fact we are honoured to be chosen to represent all the UK universities and I feel I'd better say no more unless I accidentally boast!' The Master took his seat to the murmur of appreciative chuckles.

The Prime Minister was next and, as usual, he was masterly. Bob Shaw, in Simpson's opinion, was not a polished speaker but his sense of drama and his timing were superb. In fact, he had often found polished speakers unconvincing, for they were much too smooth.

Shaw's brief speech of introduction was drawing to a close.

'I do not see you, Sir, as an Alien; I see you as a friend and one that I shall sorely miss when you journey to your distant home. I see you as a man with all the noble features of a man developed. Sir, your presence with us is a blessing. My Lords, Ladies and Gentleman – the Captain!'

The Captain rose but for a moment he said nothing. The stillness in the hall felt tangible. He smiled.

'Master, good people, what a privilege to address you in this ancient house of learning. It is also an opportunity to publicly acknowledge the care and kindness that have been lavished on us with such unstinted generosity. As for the Prime Minister, what can I say? I'll put it simply: he is a friend.'

173

The Captain bowed his head and again the hall grew still.

'I have no address prepared but I have sensed the questions in the hall. One dominates. "Why have you come?"' He paused, and Simpson sensed immediately the singleness of attention.

'We have visited your beautiful planet a number of times in the past and have studied the words of your Master Teachers, but only now have we revealed ourselves. We have drunk at the fount of this planet's wisdom and now we are here to offer back those truths in which our law is fixed. This decision to show ourselves was not taken lightly but the will of our Chief Elder prevailed. We needed to widen the fraternity of like beings, he maintained, for the Universe is single and not a thing of separateness. Our planets are special, rare if not unique amongst the heavens. There may be others, but the special conditions needed to maintain life forms such as ours are quite exacting. How did we find you? Simply, a Chief Elder, a man of great humility, told us where to look. How this is possible is beyond my ken, but in the world of Unity known to the few, that which is necessary is known.

'Humility is the door through which we may aspire to taste the Universal Goodness, but pride is ever in the wings. If you have questions, I will do my best to answer.'

A florid man sitting near the front stood up immediately.

'Sir, I'm told your views on education are authoritarian and revisionist. Is this correct?' The tone was belligerent, and Toby Simpson shifted in his seat.

'Truth is authority and this is passed through law and age-old principle. With love the teacher will convey this to the child. That which is lawful and natural will be recognised, for knowledge, and I don't mean information, is drawn out and not imposed. So-called brainwashing *is* imposed knowledge, whereas natural knowledge is natural and this the child will recognise. Children have a strong sense of fairness and, when wrongly accused, the truth arises naturally. Such a situation we may remember from our own youth.'

'We all have differing views of truth!' the questioner shot back with no little frustration.

'That, of course, is opinion, and that is why we ought to study the time-honoured principles.'

'Old fashioned...'

174

The Prime Minister, who had been whispering in the Master's ear, spoke up.

'I think, Sir, you've had your fair share!'

The man sat down with little grace.

'Next question,' the PM intoned.

'Sir, much press coverage has been given to the proposal of a location-value levy but almost all the experts I have questioned are more than sceptical. They tell me that it's completely out of step with our modern sophisticated system. How can I counter this view?'

'Natural law is never out of step and, if such a law as that pertaining to publicly created value is ignored, there will always be difficulties. Those who cite the difficulties must first study the principles, for they are self-evident. Publicly created value belongs to the public whereas privately created value, that is wages, belongs to the individual. Of course changing from the present situation would have to be gradual and a percentage would be the best one could hope for. I feel sure that, once people saw the benefits of untaxing labour, opposition would weaken. Mr Tom Wynter has been giving some excellent lectures on the subject. Those I recommend.'

'Thank you, Captain.'

The PM picked out the next questioner.

'Captain, may I ask a question on the subject of music?'

The Captain nodded.

'Just how important is music to society?'

'Vitally important.' The Captain's answer was immediate. 'Music will impose itself according to its nature. Violent music will incite violence, sensual music sensuality and sentimental music sentimentality; harmonic music brings harmony, inharmonic disharmony. It would seem to be a matter of observation and common sense, but music is close to the person, and here our likes and dislikes are strong. The ancient Greeks, as you may know, were very firm about the modes of music, but coercion doesn't work and is often counterproductive.'

Another hand shot up.

'Sir, are we to view your space vehicle before you leave? Many would be interested.'

'I must disappoint you for we are forbidden to put our technology on show. That is the law, I'm afraid.'

'How do you communicate with your planet?'

'By being very still, but I can say no more than that.'

'Thank you, Sir.' The questioner, a young man, took his seat thoughtfully.

The questions continued but Toby noted that all the speakers avoided the Captain's introduction. It was as if they were afraid to enter uncharted waters. But almost at the close a distinguished-looking man stood up to probe that very subject.

'Captain, in your opening remarks you implied an amazingly wide perspective. Can you say more on this?'

'As I hinted at the beginning, our Chief Elder is a man of remarkable humility and with him knowledge arises in a most mysterious way. To put it in analogous terms, the airways are open and instructions arise, as it were, from nowhere. For this the heart is free and open. If I said it were quite natural, you might perhaps have doubts, but the truth is always simple. Things simply happen when one is connected, for the Universe is one, not many. In fact, caring for the Universe is natural when one is universal.'

'Thank you, Sir, I am honoured to have met you.'

This was the moment to bring proceedings to a close and Toby knew the moment for his summing up.

The Prime Minister spoke first and, predictably, his final words were brief. After an equally brief introduction, Toby rose. Amazingly, he was completely calm.

'Even though I see the Captain and his Deputy almost every day, I'm still astounded at their erudition – the high table seems to be their natural home. This occasion, I can reveal, was the Prime Minister's idea and I must say I baulked at the security problems, but, watching the good-natured way in which you complied with all the frisking seemed like added entertainment. We are very grateful to the Master for permitting us to use this hallowed venue; I'm sure the evening will hold a special place in our memory.'

Chapter Forty-One

Lunch was set for half past one, which allowed the Archbishop to attend the local church. It was a motley bunch but all dressed in their best attire. Ali was there with the Major and chatting to Drusilla; Freddie Sharpe was joking with Jim Billing and Tim Bates, and the Deputy was busy talking to a Middle Eastern lady whom Toby hadn't seen before – of course she was the one who had been transformed by the the aura round the Deputy. He recognised the New Zealand newsman who was in animated conversation with the fierce-eyed cleric and the dark-suited Iranian Ambassador. The Prime Minister was there, of course, deep in conference with the Captain. Where was Tom Wynter? Ah, with his brother Richard and Lizzie. Bill was standing with his son and Toby walked across to join them.

'Did you go to Church with the Archbishop, Bill?' he asked the boy.

'I did, Sir. The Archbishop spoke very well!'

'That's known as getting in on the ground floor!' Toby winked at the father and they both laughed.

Tables were laid out in the open air with generous trays of sandwiches set out in a very English fashion. Both white and red wine were available, and tea as well. Toby chose tea.

'Tom,' he called, beckoning Tom Wynter, 'the Captain gave you a mention at Balliol. So you're up there!'

'I know, people used to ignore me totally, now my dairy's chock-a-block!'

'Toby, the Captain wants you – he's waving!'

'That's unusual – there must be something in the wind. He called the meeting: all his specials, he said. I'd better go!'

The Captain wanted everyone together inside for a brief meeting. Four chairs were placed in front. This happened easily but the sense of anticipation was obvious. At the front the Captain and his Deputy took the middle seats, with the Prime Minister and Simpson at either side. When the buzz had settled down it was the Deputy who spoke.

'Good people, we've had news from our planet. Our Chief Elder has passed on and the Captain has been chosen as his successor. Unfortunately this means that we will be returning soon. The appointment is not official until the ceremony is completed and the Captain would prefer that you continue to address him as before.'

For a time there was silence for the shock of the announcement had taken most by surprise. The Prime Minister, however, felt it incumbent on him to say appropriate words. These were echoed by a number in the gathering until eventually the Captain spoke again.

'We will miss you all,' he said simply. He bowed his head briefly. 'All of you have been touched by the Supreme. Look after one another; keep in touch, for in your various fields you will need the support of like and sympathetic minds. When we've gone Toby Simpson will take the central role. Refer to him any question you may have. How long? The answer is a week today. That is all, so I suggest we return to the garden. Get to know each other, you have all afternoon!'

Toby Simpson was shocked. Even though he had anticipated the return, he certainly hadn't anticipated the quasi-guru role. The others were beginning to move out into the garden but he still sat, reflective and unmoving. He looked up. Before him was the Captain and Drusilla.

'Let's go for a walk, Toby.'

'Yes, Sir.'

They had been walking in silence for some time before the Captain began to speak.

'Toby, I know that you have seen me standing quietly on the roof at sunrise but you have never raised the question. Your discretion is very English!' The Captain chuckled. 'I was listening, not with the ears, of course, but with the inner mind, for potent thoughts from home. It's a facility we have and you have too, but still to be developed. It's a question of being alerted to what's already there quite naturally. I should have told you of this earlier but I didn't anticipate this sudden summons.'

'This central role, Sir, has rather thrown me. What do you actually mean?'

'Both of you will have a part to play. People will come to you to talk things over. Unless asked, be slow to give advice but always listen with complete attention, for that attention is the one attention and your listening magnifies potential. It is simple, for truth is always simple.'

'I feel we ought to keep your leaving secret, for I fear unwanted attention. So I suggest we caution all the people here.'

'As you wish, Toby.'

'And your craft, Sir – would the lawn be big enough?'

'No, we would need to borrow the field next door.'

'That could be arranged. The farmer could talk, of course, but we'll deal with that. Here's the PM, Sir.'

'Captain, I've just remembered, the Russian President's visit is embarrassingly close to your departure.'

'How close, Prime Minister?'

'The day before.'

'We'll leave on Monday. That will keep Sunday free to see Her Majesty.'

'Toby, we'll have to confirm that,' the PM interjected.

Drusilla felt a strong sense of unreality. Here she was walking with the Captain, Toby and the Prime Minister in the now familiar grounds of the Manor and in only ten days' time the Captain would be gone, and Winkfield too, for it would cease to be the centre of attention.

'Drusilla, you like it here, I've heard,' the Prime Minister said, jerking her into the present.

'Yes, I'm helping Toby's secretary. There always seems to be plenty to do.'

'Well, there certainly will be plenty in the coming week. Heavens! I'd almost forgotten. It's the Indian President tomorrow.'

'What time is he arriving, Sir?'

'The afternoon.'

'Captain, India has always held a special place in our affections. We called her the jewel in the crown.'

'Oh yes, I've been reading all about it, and their amazing Scriptures.'

'Toby, I hope the President's been warned!' the PM quipped.

The Captain laughed.

Chapter Forty-Two

Sir James Huntington, on an extended tour of the East, was hosted by the Indian President on his Air India flight to London. They had ample time to chat and Sir James was most impressed by the Indian leader's spiritual insight. Certainly he knew his Gita, both Sanskrit and English, and the Foreign Secretary was confident that the meeting at Winkfield would be successful.

He was right. The Captain and the Indian President were soon engrossed and had to be reminded of the break for tea. Later they parted warmly, with Sir James escorting the President to Windsor for dinner with the Queen.

Sir James was exhausted; the extended tour and the requirements of office when he returned were almost too much. It was time to potter in the Cotswolds. This was the message he would give the PM when his friend returned from Scotland.

A surprise visit from the US Secretary of State, however, didn't give him much respite, for it was off again to Winkfield with the Secretary who was charged with delivering President Gilmore's good wishes to the Captain on his imminent departure. Clearly the PM had alerted the President and the Secretary's visit was his answer – a generous response much appreciated by the Captain and his Deputy. The Visitors were obviously moved by the messages of good-will, including those of the three Commonwealth leaders. But at the entrance security was just as tight. Dark forces were ever active.

Although one of the first to be invited, heavy, long-standing commitments had prevented the Russian President from attending earlier. But Saturday arrived and the President of the Russian Federation at last touched down at London Airport. Security, of course, was total.

The initial meeting between the Captain and the President was formal and scrupulously correct, but when the Captain began speaking in Russian, albeit not so fluent as his English, the powerful Russian melted; and later, when the Captain quoted Tolstoy, the President of all the Russias was completely won over and conversation flowed with hardly any need whatever for interpreters.

Later that evening, when the President kept a dinner appointment at Downing Street, Shaw was amazed at the openness of one who'd always walled himself with Russian pride.

The Captain had achieved much, much more than surface evidence revealed. Indeed, in the case of the Russian President, even the surface evidence was eloquent. The gathering of the previous Sunday had not included many VIPs, but the nonentities of today are the VIPs of tomorrow, and so-called nonentities are often very influential. In all, the Visitors had met many people; there'd been a constant stream. Who could tell what seeds were sown, for often it was the most unlikely person who stooped to lift the baton.

*

The Queen with the Duke arrived on Sunday after Church. The Prince of Wales was abroad and had sent a long e-mail to Toby Simpson's secretary.

The Sovereign dispensed with all formality, and enjoyed a light Sunday lunch. She asked the Captain about the animals on his planet and was interested to hear what creatures had been domesticated. The creatures, she learned, were strangely similar to ours.

'Your horses, Ma'am, are much more noble and, as here, our dogs are faithful. I must say your cats are more cuddly!'

The Queen chuckled.

'I would love to visit your planet, Captain, but alas British Airways doesn't have a service!'

They laughed, after which the Captain suggested a short circuit of the garden. This proved not so short as Her Majesty still pursued her questions. Toby was grateful for in one sense he had learned more about the Captain's planet in an afternoon than in a month of constant contact.'

They returned to their seats to find afternoon tea things laid out and ready. The Queen was clearly pleased and, on a signal from Drusilla, the teapots arrived.

The Queen's mood changed.

'My son is more than sorry to miss your send-off, Captain. We all are truly grateful for your visit and how you've lifted the level of discussion and awareness. I for my part find your company most delightful but also, Sir, you lend your peace.'

Toby just managed to control his emotion. The Queen had spoken beautifully.

*

After the Queen left, the Captain spent the rest of the day with Toby and Drusilla. He spoke little and when he did he centred on the need for stillness.

'Stillness is not created; it's not an activity or the product of one. One can connect, but even that connection is unnecessary. Stillness is the *is*-ness, the now, the presence. But all these words can act to dim perception.

'Sounds are swallowed up in stillness; watch and you will see. Physical stillness is the beginning, but the stillness that passes understanding has no beginning. This is rest; the deep rest from which all knowledge and activity arise.'

They sat for a long time without speaking. At one time Drusilla would have found this awkward and unnatural but after two weeks at Winkfield it was easy. The peace had no need of addition. She knew that Toby was very still, as was the Captain, but that did not disturb. There was no need for commentary.

Toby broke the silence, yet it didn't seem that anything was disturbed.

'Sir, looking through the window there, I had a strange affinity with the trees. It was as if I were the trees. Is this imagination?'

'The witness is single, Toby. Your great Teacher says, "Lift a stone and I am there." That "I am" is the witness, and the witness and the stillness are one. Such is the supreme simplicity.'

Drusilla was amazed. She was a Classics scholar and, in theory, all this was implied by the Greek Masters, but she had never considered it a tangible reality.

The Captain chuckled.

'This life is a great play. Let's have tea!'

Chapter Forty-Three

It was a beautiful morning; the sky was clear. It was a perfect setting for the Visitors' departure. The old grandfather clock had just struck nine and the PM had arrived. Soldiers ringed the adjacent field but so far the Visitors' craft had not arrived.

Seeing the PM and Mrs Shaw talking to the Captain and his Deputy, Toby went out into the garden. The space vehicle was due but not overdue. He turned away and looked towards the entrance but all was quiet. For the first time for over two months no visitors were expected. There was a sudden rush of air, then something like a summer squall. Instinctively he turned towards the field to see a wall of shimmering emptiness where there had been uninterrupted countryside. The Visitors' transport had arrived.

It was at least a thirty-acre field, but the invisibility shield was not dwarfed – quite the contrary, it was substantial.

In ones and twos the Visitors emerged with their modest baggage and there they waited in a bunch until the Captain and the Deputy emerged. Then the household staff who had been virtual prisoners during their stay came out to say good-bye. Tears were common, for a bond of trust and friendship had been forged. The young men and cadets filed off through what had been a hastily constructed gate, towards the shimmering screen. One by one they disappeared, swallowed by the force-field wall. Next the Deputy took his leave with his usual dignity. At last it was the Captain's turn.

'I told the Deputy that we'd let the four of you have a peek. This we see as a special gesture of appreciation, but we must not let you through the doors. That is strictly forbidden. You will feel a slight tingling as you pass through but that is all. The harsher deterrents have been temporally switched off.

The craft was much bigger than Toby had dreamed. It was not unlike the famous fictional creation, but the hull was oval with a pointed nose. In fact no feature was flat on for all was fashioned to deflect, and if there were engines they were wonderfully concealed.

'Good people, should something slip your tongue about this, it would be of little matter for the secrets are within. We simply try to keep the buzz of speculation dormant. What can I say that has not been said already? In truth, we are as one, and parting is a dream. I should retreat a little now and, ladies, hold on to your hats!'

With that the Captain disappeared within.

They all withdrew towards the screen as the giant ship lifted off soundlessly. The only noise was the rushing of the wind.

Unashamedly, tears coursed down Toby's cheeks.

'Just a moment ago he was standing amongst us and now he's gone,' he whispered.

Drusilla squeezed his hand.

'He said that parting was a dream,' she said quietly.

'Thanks, Drusilla.'

'Toby,' the PM said briskly, 'Sir James is tired and wants to retire to his cottage. Would Foreign Secretary interest you?'

Toby Simpson laughed.

'Sir, you are impossible!'